8

A DIFFERENT KIND OF CAMOUFLAGE

CORINNA TURNER

PRAISE FOR CORINNA TURNER'S BOOKS

LIBERATION: nominated for the *Carnegie Medal Award 2016*
ELFLING: 1st prize, Teen Fiction, *CPA Book Awards 2019*
I AM MARGARET & *BANE'S EYES:* finalists, *CALA Award 2016/2018*
LIBERATION & *THE SIEGE OF REGINALD HILL:* 3rd place, *CPA Book
Awards 2016/2019*

Corinna Turner was awarded the **St. Katherine Drexel Award** in **2022.**

PRAISE FOR *ELFLING*

I was instantly drawn in

EOIN COLFER, author of *Artemis Fowl* and former Childrens Laureate
of Ireland

PRAISE FOR *A DIFFERENT KIND OF CAMOUFLAGE*

*This next installment of Turner's unSparked series, with its well-developed
story world, provides unique insights into what foster children might
experience when they are placed into homes so different from all that
they've known.*

THERESA LINDEN, author of *Battle for His Soul*

*The adventure continues! Corinna Turner has done it again in her
UnSPARKed series, this time moving the action into the city, where her
characters face a different kind of danger. Separated and helpless at the
hands of the city foster-care system, Darryl and Harry must overcome
callous bureaucrats and their own inner doubts as they wonder about the
fate of their dear friend. Corinna has managed to give readers a
compelling glimpse into the life of a foster child in a future where
dinosaurs roam the earth. With moving characters and believable world-
building, her latest installment adds a whole new level of depth to this
wonderful series.*

ANTONY BARONE KOLENC, author of The Harwood Mysteries series

*In this installment, Darryl and Harry meet new challenges, and we finally
get to learn what life inside the fenced cities is like! I particularly enjoyed
the way Harry fights to maintain his identity and his integrity, despite the
difficulties he encounters.*

MARIE C. KEISER, author of *Heaven's Hunter*

ALSO BY CORINNA TURNER:

I AM MARGARET series
For older teens and up

Brothers *(A Prequel Novella)**
1: I Am Margaret*
1: Io Sono Margaret (Italian)
2: The Three Most Wanted*
3: Liberation*
4: Bane's Eyes*
5: Margo's Diary*
6: The Siege of Reginald Hill*
7: A Saint in the Family*
'The Underappreciated Virtues of Rusty
Old Bicycles' *(Prequel short story) Also
found in the anthology:*
Secrets: Visible & Invisible*

I Am Margaret: The Play *(Adapted by
Fiorella de Maria)*

UNSPARKED series
For tweens and up

Main Series:
1: Please Don't Feed the Dinosaurs
2: A Truly Raptor-ous Welcome
3: PANIC!*
4: Farmgirls Die in Cages*
5: Wild Life
6: A Right Rex Rodeo
7: FEAR
8: A Different Kind of Camouflage
9: A Different Kind of Freedom

Prequels:
BREACH!*
A Mom With Blue Feathers[†]
A Very Jurassic Christmas*
'Liam and the Hunters of Lee'Vi'

FRIENDS IN HIGH PLACES series
For tweens and up

1: The Boy Who Knew (Carlo Acutis)*
2: Old Men Don't Walk to Egypt (Saint
Joseph)*
3: Child, Unwanted (Margaret of
Castello)*

Do Carpenter's Dream of Wooden
Sheep? *(Spin-off, comes between 1 & 2)*

1: El Chico Que Lo Sabia (Spanish)
1: Il Ragazzo Che Sapeva (Italian)

YESTERDAY & TOMORROW series
For adults and mature teens only
Someday: A Novella*
Eines Tages (German)
1: Tomorrow's Dead[†]

OTHER WORKS

For teens and up
Elfling*
'The Most Expensive Alley Cat in London'
(Elfling prequel short story)

For tweens and up
Mandy Lamb & The Full Moon*
The Wolf, The Lamb, and The Air Balloon
(Mandy Lamb novella)

For adults and new adults
Three Last Things *or* The Hounding of Carl
Jarrold, Soulless Assassin*
A Changing of the Guard
The Raven & The Yew[†]

[†] Coming Soon
*** Awarded the Catholic Writers Guild *Seal of Approval*￼**

CONTENTS

HARRY

The police car tears along the highway, far too fast. They're probably not actually speeding, but every turn of the wheels carries us closer to the city and further from the Habitat Vehicle that's been our home for almost a year. Josh's beloved HabVi. What will the city-folk do with it?

Darryl moved into the center seat ages ago, so she could put her arm around me. The cop in the passenger seat turned around and fussed about her putting the seatbelt on, then left us alone again. I feel like a big baby, letting her hold me like this when I'm fourteen and near-as-nevermind a man—at least as farmers and hunters judge such things—but I can't bring myself to object. I'm trying not to think about it, but I know they'll probably split us up once we reach the city.

We've said three Chaplets of Saint Desmond, end-to-end, for Josh—and yeah, a little for us, too. Darryl has Josh's rosary; I've no idea why. Heck, Josh looked desperately ill when they took him away, that T. rex bite in his shoulder so horribly infected. Has the ambulance reached Exception City yet? Will they even manage to save him?

Darryl fell silent when we finished the last chaplet instead of starting another, carefully pocketing the beads. Thinking, I guess. My mind just echoes, emptily.

Finally, she speaks, very softly. "Harry, they're going to ask us a lot of questions about why we ran away with Josh when Fernanda tried to take us in-city last year, after Dad appeared to have been killed. We need to decide what to tell them."

I turn my head to peer at her, speaking just as quietly. "Tell them? We tell them we just didn't want to live in-city, right? We can't mention to the police about Dad being kidnapped in case the kidnappers kill him."

Darryl shakes her head, her face tight. "Harry, when we decided to flee the state to get away from Jason's vengeance for what we did to that illegal rex farm of his, we accepted that Dad was near-certain dead by now. The fact that we got caught before we could go doesn't change that. It's too late for Dad. We have to tell the truth. All of it."

"What? Why? Why risk it—?"

"*Josh,* Harry. They're going to try him for

'kidnapping' us. The more good reasons we can show he had for letting us come work for him despite the fact he was eighteen and we weren't, the more lenient they may be to him. Crazy farm kids not wanting to live in-city should prove that he didn't *kidnap*-kidnap us—but having a serious, extra-good reason, like thinking our dad would get killed if we went in-city, has to look even better, right?"

"They'll say we should have told the police at the time."

"Even if they insist we should have, I think they'll understand why we didn't."

I'm silent for a moment, watching the slushy, muddy landscape pass without seeing it. Finally, I protest, "We'll be giving up our last chance of ever getting Dad back, Ryl."

"They'll send Josh to *prison*, Harry." Her face is hard. "And they arrested Father Ben too, unless you didn't notice. *I'm* telling them the truth. You should too. It will look better if we're both saying the same thing."

"We could just omit it. Josh has always supported our efforts to get Dad back; he's always been willing to—"

"Yeah, he's sacrificed *everything* for us, Harry." Her whisper is so fierce and intense I pull back slightly. "Dad is *dead*, okay? We have to help *Josh* now, any way we can."

Angrily, I shrug free of her arm, turning toward the window, stomach churning. It's not exactly that I think she's wrong, but...*Dad*. How can I let him go? Do anything to harm him?

Darryl's voice echoes in my mind as we drive.

Dad is dead. I'm *telling them the truth.*

Josh or Dad? What do I do?

Saint Des, help me!

DARRYL

By the time we reach the city fence, Harry has allowed me to put my arm around him again, which I'm glad of, since I'm horribly afraid they're going to separate us when we get in there.

We twist and turn through bleak city streets for a while, travelling between towering skyscrapers, before pulling up outside what appears to be the central police station. The officers get us out of the car and walk us inside. Kiko cowers on my shoulder, frightened by the strangeness of it all, his four feathered wing-limbs hunched around him.

A couple of cops bring our bags, and we're installed in a corner of the waiting room, which smells of coffee and vomit. The glamorous city. Right.

"How's Josh?" I ask the junior cop who was traveling in the passenger seat, but he just shrugs and spreads his hands. Doesn't know and doesn't care to find out, clearly.

I'm surprised Fernanda Matthews isn't here already, waiting to claim us. Loathing burns in my throat at the thought of her. No, when she arrives, I *have* to stay calm. The worse I behave, the less chance I'll have of staying with Harry—or even being allowed to see him.

I remember that night, though, our last evening at home on the farm, almost a year ago. We were so happy to be alive, happy to be back safe, happier than we had any right to be, perhaps, after the double tragedy of losing Dad and Carol. But we were home, and we'd found Josh, and he'd brought hope that Dad was actually alive. *Hope*, that was what we felt. Hope for the future. Hope, warmth, safety, companionship...

And then *she* came.

The woman who's just walked through the main doors of the police station and turned toward us. She's wearing turquoise again. A frilly turquoise suit. Neat little pumps on her feet—also turquoise.

She hurries over, a look of relief on her face, her arms spread as though she thinks she's our savior, cloying apple perfume wafting our way.

"Darryl, Harry, thank goodness! It's so wonderful to have you safe at last!"

Darryl says absolutely nothing, her body rigid. I shoot her a glance. From the way her lips are pressed together, she doesn't trust herself to speak. I can't think of anything to say either, so I stay quiet too.

"Ah, good." The junior cop who's been sitting silently nearby jumps to his feet. The journey here was enough to convince him that we didn't want to chat— not to him. "We can get them signed over to you straight away, Ms. Matthews."

"Have they been good?" she inquires in that sickly sweet way that's just as horrible as I remember.

"Oh, yes. No trouble. Well, there was a little struggle back at the scene, with the girl trying to reach her abductor as he was being taken away, and the boy trying to keep some raptor chick. But other than that, they've been perfectly obedient."

Fernanda's eyes have gone very wide, her gaze fixed mostly on Darryl. "Oh, you poor *things*. Such trauma. Don't worry, Darryl, sweetie-pie. We will get you to a counselor as soon as we can. And, Harry, you too, you're safe now. No raptors will be getting anywhere *near* you."

That's too much. "No, they *misfiring* well won't," I snap, "when that *short-circuiting* monster of a cop threw our few-day-old chick into the bushes to *die!*"

"*Language*, Harry! Dear me, that awful hunter has

had a terrible influence on you."

I open my mouth, but Darryl's fingers bite into my arm. Yeah, okay. Self-control. The number one hunter virtue. Guess I'd better start acting a bit more hunter-ish—the way she is. And Josh rarely swears. I'm letting him down.

I close my mouth again.

DARRYL

Fernanda's eyes narrow on Kiko. "No pets, Darryl, sweetie-pie, remember? I'd better give someone a call about the..er...*creature*..."

Someone. The pound, no doubt.

"He's a *quadravian*—or microraptor if you want the scientific name. And it's fine," I add quickly. "I already arranged for someone to come and collect him. They'll be here soon." Will they? Uncle Mau could get here in about this time, but there's no telling when he saw that message, if he could drop everything, and how long it will take him to find out where we are. I can only try to delay.

"Hmm. Well, if they're not here by the time we have to leave, the creature will have to be taken elsewhere, at least for now."

I swallow. How long will the pound keep him, even if someone is supposed to be coming to collect him?

There'll be a long line of people wanting to adopt an exotic pet like a quadravian.

Come on, Uncle Mau. Please!

Tempting to think that something has to go right for us, soon, but I know better than that. It's perfectly possible that everything will keep on going worse and worse. And we'll never know why, until we die and ask God.

I check my pocket for Josh's dad's rosary. Still safe. I took it to try and make sure it didn't go astray, but now I'm terrified *I'll* lose it.

I thought the paperwork would take ages and give Mau time to arrive, but after only a few minutes bending over a desk, Fernanda's tip-tapping toward us again in her neat little shoes. My heart sinks.

"Okay, children, all done! Let's be on our way and get you settled in. Pick up your bags." She claps her hands like a nursery school teacher in a movie. "We'll drop Harry off first and then we can drop the pet off next."

My stomach clenches up into a knot. *Drop Harry off...* They *are* separating us. I expected it, but it still hits me like a physical blow.

And they wonder why we ran.

Harry stares at me, his face pale and strained. I pick up both my bags in one hand so I can slip an arm around him and give him a squeeze. Swallowing hard, he picks up his bags too and we follow Fernanda to the door.

"There we are, just over there," chirps Fernanda, pointing toward a little car that I recognize but wish I'd never, ever laid eyes on. "In you go, now."

She opens the trunk. Reluctantly—for want of any other option—I put my bags in, and so does Harry. Harry's just got into the car when a large shiny silver truck pulls into the parking lot much faster than most cars usually approach a police station, then swerves, screeching to a halt right beside us.

"Uncle Mau!" I gasp as the door opens and a stocky middle-aged man jumps out, enfolding me in a hug in an instant. "Uncle Mau, you made it!"

He holds me tight and I cling to him, fighting not to break down as Kiko scrambles up to the top of my head, out of the way. A whiff of familiar farm smells—sweat, and iggy dung, and Maurice Carr—sweep me back to my childhood. He didn't even stop to shower before making the journey, although he was travelling unSPARKed.

"Uncle Mau!" Harry's made it back out of the car, throwing himself on us.

Mau wraps Harry into the hug too. Right now, a hug from Mau is the next best thing to a hug from Dad. I could've really used a hug from Dad, right now. *Never again...*

"Ah, Harry, you've grown so much!"

I look up at Mau as he finally eases his grip. His face is thinner than I remember, his hair graying at the temples and receding slightly. I guess this year has been rough on him, too. He lost his best friend, misplaced his best friend's children, who he was supposed to be responsible for, and had a whole extra farm to run, which is no joke long-term, even with our other neighbors Riley and Sandra doing half. To say nothing of raising his own kids single-handed. Though he does have a nanny to help with that, unless he's in between them again.

"Mau, I'm so glad you're here!"

His expression firms again as he gets control of his emotions. "Well, we've got to salvage what we can. Bad enough these city-folk thinking they can take you two, without them taking this little fellow as well." He reaches above my head to stroke Kiko.

"Ah, admit it, Mau," I joke, "you just want him for Porscha and Lotus."

"Ah, you caught me!" But his grin is as forced as mine and his face sobers at once. "Seriously, Darryl, don't worry about him. The girls will take good care of him. He'll be spoiled rotten."

"I hope not. He'll get too fat to fly."

"I'll grab Kiko's things from the trunk," says Harry glumly, turning back to the car.

"Thanks, Harry." I unclip Kiko's leash and hand it to Mau, who prudently secures it to a ring on his jacket at once. Anything could spook Kiko in this strange environment and if he catches a good thermal and lands on top of a tower block, we'll never get him back.

I lift Kiko down into my arms and give him a kiss. "You're going to a very nice home, Kiko, don't you worry."

"Yes, little fellow. That's it, easy now." Mau rubs Kiko under the chin for a few moments until the little quadravian relaxes enough to climb onto his arm. "That's right..." He transfers Kiko to his shoulder as I glance around to check on Fernanda.

She's standing by the driver's door, her disapproving gaze fixed to farmer Mau, so I step a fraction closer to him and lower my voice. "Any luck with the guardianship?"

He winces. "Not yet. My lawyer said that with the two of you missing, the courts weren't even prepared to consider my case. Now that you're found, we might be able to get somewhere. But, uh..." He hesitates. "I reckon this...eleven-month escapade...won't have helped our chances."

My heart sinks, though I'm not surprised by his words.

He hesitates again. "Darryl, my girl, I'm sure right

now you're both feeling pretty mad. Hurting bad, too. And your instinct is to rebel, to defy them. Don't. The better you behave, the higher chance they'll be prepared to entrust you to any care other than the state."

"I know that." But I can't help how tense my shoulders have gone. "Harry knows that too," I add, since he's now standing beside us with Kiko's bag. "Hunters rock at self-control, y'know."

That makes him smile slightly, though he's deadly serious as he adds, "Just *try* to remember it, no matter how hard it gets."

"Come along, now," calls Fernanda. "Hand over the pet and let's be going. I want to have you settled in as soon as possible; you've had such an ordeal."

Ugh, that horrible woman. We haven't seen Mau for a year and she can't even give us a few minutes.

But, remembering Mau's cautions, I simply smile at him. It wobbles, badly. "Well, we'd better say goodbye."

Harry says nothing. Maybe his voice will do more than wobble if he opens his mouth.

Mau stares at the two of us, his brows drawing together in pain, and reaches out to grip our shoulders. "Ah, you two," he speaks in a low voice. "You have no idea how much I wish I could just put the two of you in my truck, right now, and take you home."

My eyes sting, but I refuse to let the tears fall. Hunters don't cry during a crisis. "If it's as much as we want you to, then we do."

But there's a whole building of cops that would take issue with that, and we all three know it.

"I'll light a fire under my lawyer," Mau promises. He gives each of us a quick, tight hug, then gets carefully into the truck with Kiko. I take the bag from Harry and put it into the back seat, then watch as Mau finishes securing the leash to the passenger seat.

"There we go. He can travel safely there."

For a moment, Harry and I look at Mau in silence and he looks at us. It feels like some semblance of normal life is so close to us we could almost—

"Chop-chop, children," chirps Fernanda.

"Guess I'd better hit the road," says Mau, closing the door at last.

"Bye, Mau," I say. "Bye, Kiko."

He starts the engine.

"Bye, Uncle Mau," squeaks Harry.

Mau shakes his head once more, in helpless regret— and drives away. We both watch his truck until it turns a corner and disappears from sight. It makes me feel more alone than ever, and they haven't even separated us yet.

HARRY

Part of me can't believe Uncle Mau just drove off without us, even though I know he had no choice. It just doesn't seem...natural. We should be with him, not left *here*.

Darryl is silent as we get into the little car. Fernanda's apple perfume is even more over-powering in the confined space. Darryl sits in the back with me rather than beside Fernanda, gripping my hand tightly again. I can't believe they're going to split us up. Well, I can, because they were before, but...

If only Uncle Mau *could* get custody of us. Until Darryl turns eighteen, in six months' time, that's probably our only chance of getting out of the city.

Is Josh okay? What chance has *he* got of getting out of the city any time soon?

We're heading out of the city center, toward the suburbs. An expensive area, I guess, since the tall blocks of apartments are giving way to those shorter stepped buildings where each floor has its own balcony or garden area. They look like long horizontal staircases or—what are those ancient things?—ziggurats, that's it.

Fernanda pulls up outside a little garden with a white fence, in front of one of the blocks. "Here we are, Harry. The Jeffords are a lovely couple. I'm sure you'll be very happy here."

Panic explodes inside me. "Isn't it temporary? Until

you find me a placement with Darryl?"

Fernanda turns in her seat, directing a dubious look at Darryl. "I'm afraid your sister will be going to a secure placement, at least until we can be sure she doesn't pose a flight risk. Which could take a while after these...unfortunate events."

Darryl bites her lip. She doesn't speak.

"Come along, Harry." Fernanda's all chirpy again as she turns and opens her door. "Out we get."

This is my last chance to ask... "Ms. Matthews, do you know if Josh is okay?"

She turns around again, her face grim, eyes darting from Darryl to me. Even with that grim face, she still coos at us. "In the circumstances, it is best that neither of you are exposed to further information about that man. It's very important that you try not to think about him except when speaking with trained professionals, okay?"

What?

"But...how *is* he?" I persist.

"Don't think about him, Harry, dear. You'll never have to see him again. Now, come along and meet the Jeffords." She gets out of the car and opens the back door and the trunk. Reluctantly, I get out and remove my bags.

"Just wait here, Darryl, dear," chirps Fernanda. "We won't be long." She slams the car door and two little beeps says she's double-locked it.

Flight risk. Right. They really think Darryl's just gonna run off and leave me here in-city by myself? I can imagine Josh shaking his head and muttering, "City-folk," the way he does.

"Is Josh okay?" I demand, following Fernanda along the garden path.

She tuts. "I just told you, Harry, it is not in your and your sister's best interests to be exposed to anything concerning that man. You need to put this whole ordeal behind you and move on."

"The only ordeal was being kidnapped and brought in-city by the police," I mutter, though not very loud. I don't want to make things harder for Uncle Mau's lawyer. Hopefully he's got a good lawyer. He's rich, right? Better off than Dad, anyway. Okay, so the night before last wasn't much fun, when Josh got injured, but that was the kidnappers' fault, for making our attempted rescue necessary. Being brought in-city is a totally different pen of piranha'saurs.

The man and woman on the porch are both fairly light-skinned although the woman has quite a far eastern look, especially around her eyes. They beam at me as though I'm about six. Again I hear Josh's voice. *City-folk*.

"Harry, this is Susannah and Philip Jefford. They're going to be your foster parents." Fernanda turns her attention to them. "This is Harry. I'm so sorry, but is it okay if I head straight off? I don't want to leave his sister unattended for long. She's being ever so good, but that was how she tricked me last time..."

They nod and murmur, "Don't mention it."

Fernanda smiles and chirps, "Be good, Harry," then honest-to-God pats me on the head before hurrying back down the garden path.

"When can I see Darryl?" I shout after her, but she just flaps her hand at me and gets into the car.

I see Darryl waving to me from the back—and then it's gone.

DARRYL

"How's Josh?" I ask, as soon as we're moving.

Fernanda sighs and doesn't answer.

"Surely you can at least tell me if he's *alive*?"

"Just put him from your mind, sweetie-pie. He can't hurt you anymore."

"Josh has *never* hurt me!"

Fernanda sighs so tragically, shaking her head, that it makes me want to strangle her.

"Where are you taking me? Juvie?"

"No, dear. I'm taking you to a secure group home. You won't enjoy the liberties a girl your age normally would, but you're not actually incarcerated. You'll attend school normally."

"School? I finished my final grade certificate last month. Harry's finished for this year as well. It should be on my records."

"Be that as it may, in the circumstances, it is far preferable that you experience at least a few months of normal life before going out into the world as an adult. We have so little time to wipe out all the harm that—" She breaks off.

"How *is* Josh?" I ask.

She purses her lips and doesn't answer.

HARRY

Susannah and Philip seem nice, in a limp city-ish kinda way. Their house—apartment—is swank, everything painted white with lime-green see-through edging everywhere. The furniture, bizarrely, all matches, every single item, colors and style and everything. It's like I stepped into a magazine, not a real house. Did they buy it all at once? In the farmhouse at home, every piece has family history behind it. In fact, I hope Darryl remembers it all, because I don't. If Dad's gone...

Dad. What do I say when they ask me why we ran?

'My' room is just as magazine perfect as the rest of the house. It's gonna be like living in some kinda sterile lab. I dump my bags on the bed, disarranging the perfect lime-green and white striped cover, fighting not to cry again. I'd swap all this space for that pokey cupboard-bunk in the 'Vi in an instant.

Fortunately, my stomach chooses that moment to growl loudly and, after getting reminded to wash my hands as though I'm a little kid, we sit down for dinner—chicken casserole. Fancy. We shoot birds to eat often enough with our .22s in the 'Vi but, in-city, avian meat is pricey.

"Goodness, you're hungry," says Susannah. "Here, have some more." She ladles another portion onto my plate. I'm so busy digging in I almost miss the worried look she exchanges with Philip. What?

Oh. Think Josh was starving me, do they?

"Thanks, I missed lunch today," I say quickly. "Josh was ill and we were trying to look after him and get him to the hospital. No time to eat. We never usually miss meals."

Except on actual hunting days, of course. Then it's a mouthful of dried fruit and nuts eaten standing, if you're lucky. No need to mention that.

They exchange another look, this one slightly panic-stricken.

"Hey, do you know how Josh is doing?"

Yep, the panic increases. They've been told not to talk about him, haven't they?

"No, sorry," says Philip. "Now, how about some

dessert?"

"No, thanks, it's Lent." My plate's empty, so I put down my knife and fork. I needed that—I missed breakfast too, come to think—but, Lent or not, I wouldn't sit around scarfing down fancy city-dessert while Josh's lying at death's door and they've taken Darryl away because she's a 'flight risk' and everything stinks this badly.

And it *is* Lent, and I'm gonna keep a hunter-Lent— even if I have to be in here.

DARRYL

My heart sinks as we drive and drive. This secure group home is nowhere near Harry's place. How often will I be able to see him?

Eventually we pull up outside a building in an older part of the city, a tall, narrow terraced house. It's a fine looking building and the solid grilles covering the windows give it a homey air—except I guess they're to keep girls in, not 'saurs out.

I collect my remaining bag and follow Fernanda up the steps to a grand wooden door. No welcome committee here. What's this place going to be like? Thinking of the sorta girls that get sent here...it may be best to make a strong first impression. I'm already head to toe in typical hunter gear, khaki and camo, with sturdy boots, but... I put my bag down for a moment, unzip it, and fish out my claw necklace, looping it around my neck. Fernanda stares at the nine-inch Utahraptor claw that now forms the centerpiece and practically fans herself in horror.

"Darryl, really, what a *dreadful* thing..."

Fortunately the door opens before she can ask me to take it off. I tuck it inside my jacket, more naturally, and follow her inside.

The lady who's opened the door is short, with fair skin, dark hair, and a no-nonsense attitude. "Darryl Franklyn, I presume?"

"Yes, ma'am."

She nods firmly, as though I've made the right first impression on her.

"Good, come through to the office and let me get you on the books."

Fernanda follows us into a room where a terminal hums quietly and says breathily, "Ms. Williamson, I must warn you, she has a *very* dangerous-looking item around her neck."

Ms. Williamson fixes me with a look. "Let's see."

I fish the necklace back out again and hold it up, my heart in my mouth. Will she confiscate it?

She eyes it for a moment. "I believe those represent some sort of important cultural status symbol, in rural communities," she says at last, "so Darryl may keep it for now. One hint of it being used as a weapon, though, and it's gone." She gives me a direct stare. "Understood, Darryl?"

"Of course. It ain't a *weapon*."

"It was for the...what, a raptor?"

Guess she's right about that. "Yeah, the big one in the middle is from a Utahraptor."

"And you're tougher than the raptor because you killed it, is that how it goes?"

That's a huge oversimplification of what a claw necklace conveys, but it isn't totally wrong so I simply shrug. If the girls here understand that much and don't give me a hard time, it'll do. What would Fernanda say if she knew I had a whole *box* full of raptor claws in my bag? I gave up collecting all of them after becoming a hunter, of course; it's just my stash of good ones for handicrafting.

"Okay, let me check through your information," says Ms. Williamson, sitting at the terminal and opening a file. "Darryl Franklyn, seventeen years old, went on the run with your younger brother and an adult hunter for eleven months, just recaptured..."

Fernanda coughs delicately. "Rescued, Ms. Williamson. *Rescued*."

"Just retrieved," Ms. Williamson compromises dryly, "which is why you are here, to prevent any repeat of aforementioned dangerous gallivanting. All correct?"

"Definitely *captured* and, yes, all correct."

"Any special dietary requirements?"

"No meat on Fridays."

She nods and notes this down. I glance at Fernanda. "Oh, Harry *will* be allowed to go to Mass on Sundays, won't he?"

"Of course." Fernanda looks down her nose at me. "If he wants to, that's something his foster parents should facilitate."

"And me?"

"Well, *that* will depend on how you behave—and will be up to Ms. Williamson. Anyway, I had better be on my way. I'll be in touch as soon as possible, Ms. Williamson, about Darryl's first counseling session. Such a terrible ordeal—she must be traumatized."

"Alright, well, if you let yourself out, I'll be giving Darryl a rundown of the ground rules."

Fernanda tip-taps away in her little pumps and after a moment the front door clicks shut. Good riddance.

Ms. Williamson watches me watching Fernanda leave. "Alright, Darryl. I've had a few hunter girls here before, although never a farmer, but I've got some idea what I'm dealing with. You're probably one tough cookie, by city-standards, think of yourself as an adult, no patience for childish things. Probably have an excellent nose for danger in some areas but are absolutely clueless in others. So to cover the most likely point of ignorance straight off, *do not be alone with boys.* Especially any boys the girls here introduce you to. I can't put it more plainly than that."

I'm wary of the power this woman has over me and resent her role as my jailor, but I'm warming to her, nonetheless. She's very straight-spoken, for a city-lady.

"I do know that," I say. Do hunter-born girls *not* know that? I guess if you're raised at a decent camp, with strong, traditional rural values about that kinda thing and limited visitors, maybe that's not something you've ever had to worry about. Why would you end up here, though? Well, how did I?

"Yet, according to your file, you ran away with a young man you'd known for about twenty-four hours, correct?"

"It wasn't like that," I say wearily. Why will no one believe us? Actually, the hunter Elders did take Josh's word for it, at the midwinter fair. "Anyway, Harry was with us. And if you'd actually *met* Josh, it wouldn't worry you, neither."

"Very well, but I'd like a little more caution from you now you're in the city. You country folk seem to operate by different standards, so you could easily get caught out."

I nod, so she goes on, "House rules are simple. No

violence, no drinking, no illegal activities, no sneaking boys in, no bullying. Okay?"

"You have to have actual rules against those things in-city?" The sarcasm slips out, but fortunately she just gives a dry smile.

"I'm afraid you'll be under full restrictions to begin with, until you prove yourself trustworthy. You'll travel to and from school with your roommates, no deviating. Supervised visits from relatives only. Shopping, initially in company of a staff member only. Relaxations can come swiftly if you behave. And seriously, stay away from gangs."

Come on, even a country-girl knows *that*! "Can I go to Mass?" The only tiny silver lining of being in-city is the possibility of Mass every single Sunday.

"Unless you misbehave, yes."

"When can I see Harry?"

"His foster parents will need to arrange a supervised visit at a time when they are able to bring him."

"Do you know if Josh is alive?"

Her strict expression softens slightly. "I'm very sorry, Darryl, but even if I knew, I am not allowed to tell you. Your caseworker—that's Ms. Matthews—has complete oversight of your emotional and psychological rehabilitation."

"What the heck does that mean? Brainwashing me

into a city-girl?"

"I dare say she'll give it her best shot. But you'll only be with us for six months, so it's a waste of time, in my opinion. You do not look especially traumatized to me."

I swallow a snort of laughter with difficulty. Yeah, this woman is not so bad.

"Alright, unless you have any more questions, I'll take you to your room. Oh, one more thing. Some of the girls here may not come across very favorably to you. They may seem mean, cold, even cruel. I've seen your file; you were raised in a stable family home. Most of them weren't. Just bear that in mind when you judge them. Alright, come with me."

Ms. Williamson points out a dining room at the rear of the ground floor, and what she calls the 'parlor' at the front—that's where the supervised visits take place. Apparently there's a big kitchen downstairs that's out of bounds to girls. The main staircase is as grand as the front door, though the floor is covered in utilitarian linoleum and everything appears to be very firmly fixed in place. On the next floor, Ms. Williamson shows me the games room, a study room and a kitchenette, all for the use of the girls. At the top of another, smaller, staircase is a corridor with six doors. The one closest to the stairs, she tells me, is her room, the others are bedrooms for the inmates...sorry, girls.

"All girls here are over fourteen," she says. "The home is for girls who are too big a flight risk to place with foster families but who haven't been sentenced to juvie."

She stops outside the third room along and raps firmly on the door, then opens it.

"Hello, girls. This is Darryl, who will be joining you."

I follow her inside. There's a bunk bed on each side of the room, with a window in between, and two dressers, complete with mirrors and chairs just to each side of it. Along the wall beside the door are four large metal cupboards, with locks on. Guess those are for our stuff.

Three girls are already in the room. One lounges on a bottom bunk, holding a physical magazine with movie stars on the cover, while two sit in the chairs, facing each other. The girl in the bunk might be my age, but the other two look slightly younger.

"This is Kerri." Ms. Williamson indicates the girl on the bed, who stares at me over her magazine. "Marnie and Fei." She indicates the other two girls.

"Hi," I say, trying to sound very calm and casual. If I get off on the wrong foot with these girls, they can make my life miserable for the next six months, stupid to pretend they can't.

"Hi," says Fei. She and Marnie are both fair-skinned. Fei has blond hair, while Marnie's is red. Marnie just goes on looking at me silently, like she doesn't talk much.

Kerri still stares—flatly. I guess she's summing me up. She's got African American features and is quite dark-skinned, about the same shade as Josh's almost-uncle, West, but lighter than Father Ben. Since we're close in age, she may see me as a threat to her position in the pack. As it were.

"Well, I'll leave you to settle in." Ms. Williamson withdraws, closing the door behind her.

I eye the beds. Three of them have patterned duvets, but the second top bunk—over Kerri—has a plain one. I move toward it. "Is this my bunk?"

Fei nods. They all look intimidated by me—which is what I wanted, of course, but I don't want to take it too far.

"That's nice," I say. "I had a top berth at home."

"Berth?" queries Fei.

"It was a HabVi."

Fei's eyes move to my necklace, as though she only now dares to show interest in it. "That's why you've got claws around your neck. You're a hunter."

"Sure am."

Am I? Hunter or farmer? I guess I've a right to claim to be either, now.

I put my bag on my bed, then climb up and unzip it.

Although I've simply been wearing clean clothes to bed for months now, the way hunters do, I still have my pajamas from the farm so I tuck those under the duvet, ready for later. There's a small lockable box just over the head of the bed, so I move my little photo album and paperwork—birth certificates and so on—into that. They're only copies of the electronic originals, of course, on the state system, but they're official ones and useful to have. I lock it and pocket the key. I guess the rest of my stuff needs to go into the cupboard.

When I get down and carry the bag across the room, Fei follows after me. Marnie and Kerri still stare, fearful and considering-whether-to-be-hostile, respectively.

"Have you got anything interesting?" Fei asks hesitantly.

"I've got some hunter handicrafting stuff. Wanna see?"

"Yeah!"

The feathers and bone beads and leather soon have Marnie creeping over to look as well, and the teeth and claws finally break the ice with Kerri, who joins us when they appear.

"These are awesome!" She strokes a huge allosaur claw, fatter and stubbier than one from a raptor.

"That's from an allosaur that ate our dinner one evening."

"It *what*?" Kerri queries, still examining the claw.

"We'd just shot a bunch of rabbits. Josh—our boss—was gonna cook some of his delish pies, but this allo came out of nowhere and ate them up, every last one."

"But it didn't eat you?" asks Fei, wide-eyed.

"Nah, I was in the turret with my brother. Josh was outside, but he jumped into a patch of marsh so the allo didn't notice him. The allo was already badly injured and starving, so once it was safely away from Josh, I took it down."

"You really killed it yourself? Cool," breathes Kerri. "I wish I knew how to hunt."

There's a hard edge to her that makes me think of pain. "You can keep that claw, if you like," I tell her.

"For real?"

"Sure." I glance at Fei and Marnie. "You can both choose one too."

"Can I have this?" Fei holds up a really smooth, shiny claw.

"Sure. That's from a Dakotaraptor."

Marnie feels her way through the box for ages, before finally holding up a perfectly-shaped three-inch tooth.

"Yeah, you can have that," I tell her. "That's from the same allo as Kerri's claw."

Marnie beams, folding both hands around the tooth as though thrilled it has such a story behind it.

They watch as I transfer my few things to my

cupboard, fiddling with their loot.

"Don't you have any dresses?" demands Kerri.

"I have a few back at my original home. Just for formal occasions. But I didn't take them with me when I left to become a hunter. Not much space in a HabVi."

"What was your original home?" She's sounding fairly friendly now, though with a guarded edge that I doubt she drops with anyone.

"A farm. They tried to make us come in-city after our dad died, so we ran away to work for a hunter. Unfortunately, they finally caught us."

"Bad luck." Kerri sounds genuinely sympathetic.

"What's it like here?"

"Better than juvie. Better than either of the two foster homes I was in, actually."

"What was wrong with them?" I ask quickly. Will Harry be okay?

"First couple were just so sickly sweet I thought I'd die of a glucose overdose. Second couple were in it for the money and didn't care. Which you'd think would be better than the first place, but they took it too far, so I ran off. Did some stealing and stuff to survive and ended up in juvie, then they released me to here. Balance isn't too bad at this place, and it's better than the street. Most of the staff are decent and Ms. Williamson is firm but fair. She'll ground you, but you'll know exactly why. I'm hoping I can stay here until I'm eighteen—only another eight months."

She is younger than me—slightly.

"I've only gotta be here for six months, but that's long enough, so I'm glad it's not too bad."

A bell rings downstairs.

Fei bounces to her feet. "It's dinnertime!"

Good, despite everything, I'm ravenous. I missed both breakfast and lunch, I was so busy worrying about Josh. I quickly place the last few things into the cupboard and lock it, carefully pocketing the key. Everything's going well with my roommates so far—but I'm not that dumb.

I just wish I knew how Josh was doing.

HARRY

I lie in my clean, perfect bed, staring up at the ceiling. Which I can see really well, because light from the street outside pours around the curtains. How do city-folk sleep like this? Why don't they put up shutters? I guess they don't need what I think of as 'normal' steel shutters, like on a farmhouse or HabVi. Their first function is defense, not light-proofing. But the brightness sure is getting on my nerves.

I say a chaplet for Josh to pass the time. Susannah and Philip don't know anything, and it's clear that if they did, they wouldn't tell me. And it helps take my mind off tomorrow.

School. I'm dreading it. Darryl and I have never been to school in our lives.

Heck, I miss Darryl. And Josh. So much. But I'm not gonna cry again. I'm not.

DARRYL

Ms. Williamson turned the room lights out at ten o'clock, but it isn't remotely dark in here. So much light spilling in from the street. Why don't they get better curtains or blinds or something? Maybe city-folk don't care.

After eleven months in the 'Vi's windowless 'master bedroom' in even pitchier blackness than my room back at the farmhouse, the light's hard to ignore.

Or maybe it's my churning stomach that's hard to ignore. The rest of the evening went okay. My roommates seem ready to be friends—I guess I'm 'cool' enough to be interesting and intimidating enough to want on their side—so that's the biggest hurdle cleared. However miserable it's going to be stuck in-city for six months, I've no real doubt I can survive it. Hopefully Harry will be okay, too.

It's Josh I'm really worried about. I asked Ms. Williamson about him again at Lights Out and she didn't know anything—and made it clear she couldn't tell me if she did. How am I going to find out if he's even alive? I guess if he's alive, the police will be along to interview me at some point.

But not knowing...it's like being trapped in a nightmare.

I can take out the little photo album in my bedside box and look at pictures of Mom, Dad, Harry... But they took our ScreamerBands so I don't have even one photograph of Josh.

Josh, are you alive?

Again I see him struggling helplessly, begging them to let him go, even though the hospital was his only chance of surviving the infection...

The memory is too strong. Tears prick my eyes. No, I mustn't cry. Hunters are fairly relaxed about tears—when everything's safe and there's cause for them—but I've a feeling these city-girls will see them as a sign of weakness. But it's no good. My throat tightens and burns...

Slipping from the bed, I pad from the room, go along the corridor to the bathroom, and lock myself in. I sit on the closed toilet seat and hug myself. Josh has such a terrible fear of the city, a full-on phobia. Even if he's alive, he must be suffering terribly.

Josh, where are you?

Alone and terrified in a hospital bed? Or lying in a cold metal drawer in the hospital morgue?

That thought is too much. I just manage to get off the toilet and lift the lid before I vomit up my dinner. I clamp a piece of toilet tissue to my mouth and kneel there, sobbing as quietly as I can.

Please don't be dead. Please don't be dead. O Lord, please don't let him be dead...

HARRY

School is overwhelming. I keep to myself, though, and no one seems very interested in me. That's a relief—I guess I just couldn't wrap my head around how many kids would be here. One new boy means nothing in this throng. Each class is with a different group of kids, some the same, some new. Even the kids in my 'home room' don't seem that interested. Susannah put out some clean, new city-clothes for me to wear, and I was so nervous that I put them on.

City culture has two main streams that used to clash but nowadays mostly just rub along beside one another: rough, tough Tats—historians argue over whether that's short for tattooed or for tattered—and Tidies—that name being self-explanatory. Susannah and Philip are definitely Tidies, same as Fernanda, but even a country-boy like me knows that Tat culture is all the rage among kids my age right now. So I'm super-grateful to Susannah for providing me with the suitably ragged yellow-and-black Tat-style gear that lets me be invisible like this.

Though, *honestly?* I do kinda wish I'd worn my proper clothes—feels like I've let the city win, right now on day one—and that doesn't feel good at all.

The classes are dead boring, since I already finished up my whole year's certificate in the winter. Josh and Darryl both considered school to be about the only acceptable excuse to put down my handicrafting for a while. But apparently I still have to attend physical school, for the 'experience.' I said to Philip, "wouldn't it be better if I stayed in the house and did something useful," and he looked surprised and said, "like what?" and since I couldn't think of any city equivalent I said "make some handicrafting items to sell." And he just looked totally bewildered.

I sure aren't getting the impression from what I'm overhearing that any of these fourteen-year-olds I'm at school with do anything to contribute to their household income. Guess that's why Philip didn't understand what I was talking about.

I never did like handicrafting much, but I'd rather do some of that than wade around in this sea of city-kids. I just hope they carry on being uninterested. I feel like a baby leggy'saur in a shoal of piranha'saurs, like any moment they might all turn on me.

Good news is, Susannah said they've already

arranged for me to visit Darryl on the weekend. And Philip said he'd bring me to Mass on Sunday, even though neither he nor Susannah is religious. I sure don't want to be here, but at least they do seem to be genuinely nice—and that is something.

DARRYL

The walk to school is a little bit interesting, as Kerri and Fei point out various landmarks along the route, Marnie trailing silently. Kerri and I are in quite a few of the same classes, and she sits with me. She seems to have decided that trying to assert dominance over a crazy hunter chick is a waste of time and is keen to be friends instead, which is fine by me. Everyone else gives me a wide berth, though whether because of my camo gear or because I'm 'one of those girls from the home' I'm not sure.

The schoolwork is dull, though. My mind keeps drifting, big time…

"Ugh, Pachy ballet," says Josh, pausing on our walk through the fairground to point at a crowded arena. "Stupidest sport out there."

Josh, West, Thiago, and Ed all wait so Harry and I can climb on an empty seat to get a look over the crowd. In the arena, a hunter with a big sparkly, rustly silver cape—a survival blanket on a heavily decorated stick, by the look of it—is waving it at an irate pachysaur, then dodging at the last minute as it charges at him.

"Heck!" Pachys may be herbi'saurs and are small compared to many 'saurs, but they have immensely thick, domed skulls that they use to head butt each other with tremendous force—to say nothing of the spikes. The injuries if that thing connects with a human don't bear thinking about.

"Yeah. It's dumb as anything," says Josh. "I think people watch it just to see it go wrong. Sick, if you ask me. Come on, let's go to the proper rodeo."

What do hunters consider 'proper' rodeo? Well, I'll soon know. We're already approaching another arena...

The teacher's voice breaks into the memory.

Josh, are you okay?

Yet again I blink and drag my attention back to class, though there's not much point. I finished up my certificate in the long dark winter months; I don't need to be here. I was going to take a break until the fall. Josh took a further course in geography the winter before he met us, and although he already knows the stars really well on a practical level, he was planning to do one in astronomy next. After we showed up, he decided to delay it until he was earning normally again—further courses not being free, of course. I was gonna take it with him, if I'd earned enough.

When I get back from school with my roommates, I stick my head into Ms. Williamson's office and ask how

Josh is. She just shakes her head at me. I head to the home's phone instead. I accessed the net via a school terminal during the lunch break and took down a list of contact numbers for every hospital in the city. I start at the top and dial my way through them all—but they won't even tell me if he's been *admitted*, let alone if he's alive.

"Are you his next of kin?" the receptionists drone.

"I might as well be!" I scream at the last one, my frustration boiling over. Maybe West, Thiago, and Ed could reasonably claim that status, but they probably don't even know yet that he's ill.

When I slam the phone back into its docking cradle, a little too hard, Ms. Williamson is standing in her office doorway, watching me. "What are you doing, Darryl?"

But I'm quite sure she knows exactly what I'm doing.

"Getting nowhere," I say—and head upstairs.

HARRY

Susannah drove me to and from the school for the first two days in her little naked, grille-less city-car but, when I realized how close it was, I asked them last night if I could walk in the future. They discussed it, ever so seriously—and this morning they said I could. It's been nice to stretch my legs in the open air, even if it's all concrete and fumes. Though the streets make me nervous. *Everyone* is a stranger.

Ugh, is *everything* gonna make me nervous now? I hate this! Out in the 'Vi—or back on the farm—I felt so strong and capable and…and grown-up. I felt very much *myself*.

But, in here, I feel as helpless as a piece of thistle fluff blowing on the wind.

DARRYL

I've only been to Mass in a real church a few times, so Sunday was awesome—and Harry was allowed to sit with me, which was even better. I couldn't talk to him properly until his foster parents brought him to the parlor at the home afterward. That was awful, 'cause I had to tell him I didn't know anything about Josh. He said he wasn't surprised, but he still looked real disappointed.

Every day at school I've looked up more places to try to find information about Josh. I've even considered calling the newspapers, but I've decided not to. I'm just not sure enough they'd take Josh's side. It's day seven, now—Monday—and I've just called each hospital in turn—one receptionist hangs up at the sound of my voice—the Child Protective Services Head Office, the Police Station, and the city's mayor—can't get through to him—and finally, yet again, Fernanda's direct number.

"Darryl, sweetie-pie"—despite the endearment, there's an edge to her voice—"would you please stop calling me?"

"I thought you said to call you anytime if I needed you?" I say sweetly.

"Please stop calling me about *this*."

"I'm gonna to call you every day until you tell me if he's alive," I say levelly. "So tell me—or get used to it."

The next day I call her before school, then beg the use of a school phone and call her at lunch as well. When I get back to the home, Ms. Williamson has removed the phone handset.

I knock on the doorway of her office. "Ms. Williamson, please may I use the phone? Or your communicator?" It's worth a try.

She sighs and shakes her head. "Sorry, Darryl. Ms. Matthews' orders. No phone calls for you for a while."

I kick the doorframe and march upstairs. That *insufferable* woman!

HARRY

"How was school?" Susannah appears in the doorway of her home office, smiling brilliantly at me as I come in the door.

As boring as the previous days, would be the truthful answer. "Fine, thanks."

"Would you like a snack?"

Without waiting for my answer, she hurries into the kitchen, leaving me hovering awkwardly in the hall. I *am* hungry, but it's so weird having grown-ups waiting on me like this. Does she think I'm too young to get my own snack? I didn't cook as often as Darryl or Josh but I did *cook.* I even cooked the odd meal back on the farm! They don't seem to expect me to do *anything* around the house or garden. On day two I asked what my chores would be and just got a bewildered look. No wonder those kids at school seem to have nothing but air in their heads.

When I go into the kitchen-diner there are some crumbs on the table. Quickly, I sweep them up, putting them into the food trash.

"It's okay, Harry, I can do that later," says Susannah, looking distressed.

"*Later?* It's *food.*" Then I remember that their food trash can isn't even sealed or anything, and putting them in there won't reduce food scent in the slightest.

Susannah looks confused. "Why does that matter?"

"I guess it doesn't, in here."

"In here?"

"In-city." She still looks puzzled, so I explain, "Even on a farm, you wouldn't leave those crumbs out, because it could attract vermin. In a HabVi it might attract something far more dangerous."

A sick expression settles on her face. "You poor boy," she whispers.

"No!" I snap. "Stop *doing* that! What's so tragic about having to simply remember to clear food away promptly? Why is that a big deal?"

Her eyes widen. "But...isn't it horrible knowing what's...what's out there? Living like that? All the time..."

Her breathy voice has my temper boiling up like a geyser.

"Not as bad as walking about out *there*!" I jab my finger towards the street, then storm into my room and slam the door, throwing myself on my bed.

By the time there's a hesitant *knock-knock,* I'm feeling bad. Self-control? Not so much.

Susannah looks around the door. "Harry, I brought your snack?"

When I manage something like a smile, she beams back and hurries across to place a plate on the gleaming white bedside table.

"I'm sorry I yelled," I mutter.

Sympathy fills her eyes again. "You can't help the ordeal you've been through—"

I hold up a hand, quickly, swallowing a fresh surge of anger. They really are more clueless than anything. I guess I should try to explain before getting frustrated with them.

"Susannah, doesn't it make *your* skin crawl walking the city streets, knowing there are guys with knives lurking, maybe so desperate for the contents of your purse they'll kill you for it?"

"That's not the..." She trails off, her mouth slightly open.

Not the same?

"It creeps me out *worse*," I say, a little heat leaking into my voice. "I mean, wildlife trying to eat you is just nature being nature, but *people* hurting each other is horrible. In the countryside everyone pulls together, mostly."

Except 'shoot on sight' Jason. And the kidnappers who took Dad. But I'm not going to mention that. No one's come to interview me, yet. What will I say?

"Is there any news about Josh?" I ask.

She shakes her head. "Sorry, Harry. I did call Ms. Matthews again and asked, like I promised."

I can't believe that horrible woman won't tell me if Josh is dead or alive. Darryl must be going *crazy*. It's totally unfair.

That flame of anger flares, catching hold again. But what can I *do*? Fernanda controls me completely. I mean, she's *already* got me acting like a good little city-boy, right? Doing as I'm told, scared of my own shadow... Ugh. No. Uncle Mau can say what he likes, I can't let her win like this!

DARRYL

"Stay low," hisses Josh, making frantic down, down motions as the idiot city-guy walks up the slope merely bent at the waist and towering far too tall.

Thankfully, the guy drops to his knees to crawl the last few feet, so I turn my attention back to the raptor nesting ground well below us.

"So, which egg is it your company wants so bad?" murmurs Josh. "Can you point it out?"

"Sure, it's that big one, with the neon markings that look just like the EonDrive logo. See it?"

"Yep." Josh sweeps the clearing with his sights, taking stock of the different Utahraptors—all twelve of them, sleek-feathered and rippling-muscled—then shakes his head. "Look, I'm sorry, man, but this is nuts. This ain't some random loner pair trying to hatch an egg or two all by themselves, like you made it sound, that we could just distract for a moment. This is not happening."

"Then what did you bring me all the way out here for?" demands the city-guy, far too loudly.

Josh shoots a quick look at the raptor pack, then scowls at him. "To perform an evaluation, just like the contract said. Well, we've performed it and the answer's no. Can't be done."

"Sure it can." The guy takes on a downright wheedling tone. "You and the girl and the kid have your rifles, we've got a clear view of the raptors. Looks easy enough to me."

"It's nesting time," Josh says, his lip curling. "No killing 'em in this season."

"You'd be well paid. Real well paid. No one will ever know."

"I ain't shooting a whole pack just to get some stupid freak egg for your bosses; no way." Josh glowers at the guy. "We're going back to the HabVi now."

The city-guy opens his mouth again, angry color flooding his cheeks, but after locking eyes with Josh for a moment, he drops his gaze and shuts his mouth again. Yeah, Josh looks that inflexible.

Relief fills me as we head back down the safe side of the ridge.

"Rex nesting is bad enough," mutters Harry behind me, "with just one mother animal to distract. But raptor eggs?"

I shush him, though I agree one hundred percent.

Josh swings around suddenly, his eyes darting behind us. His brows draw together in alarm.

"Where's the suit?"

I turn, so does Harry. Heck, when did I last hear the guy scuffing his way noisily along behind Harry?

"He can't have gone after the egg by himself?" whispers Harry, wide-eyed.

"He's trying to force our hand, the fool," snaps Josh.

"Thinks we'll have to go save him."

We stand looking at each other, my stomach curdling.

"Oh, misfire," swears Josh. "If the raptors don't kill him…"

Soon we're peering down at the nest again. No sign of the suit.

"Harry, cover us," says Josh. "If we can't catch up to him before he wanders in there, he's probably a goner."

"Keep sharp, Harry," I whisper.

"And don't forget to check behind you nice and regular," adds Josh over his shoulder as we move away.

Yeah, raptors are well known for sneaking up on their prey. Despite that, I doubt Josh intends for us to actually enter the nesting ground itself—which is all Harry really has in his sights. He's just trying to leave Harry in the safest place. Fine by me.

Josh easily tracks the idiot city-man down the boulder-strewn slope and into the crags surrounding the nesting ground. But we still haven't found him by the time Josh pauses, points down the ravine we're following, lays two fingers to his arm, then places his fingertip to his lips.

He estimates we're only about two hundred feet from the nests. We mustn't make a sound. Right.

Where *is* that fool?

A terrified yell from ahead…shots from Harry's position…

The retorts continue as Josh darts forward, covering the

remaining distance at speed and peeping around an outcrop. I peer over his shoulder. The city-man is out in the center of the nesting ground, his back to a pillar of rock, blood spilling between his fingers as he clutches one arm. A couple of dead raptors lie nearby and regular shots continue to send chips of rock flying up as Harry lays down covering fire. The other raptors lurk warily around the edges of the nesting ground, their furious eyes on Suit Man, ruffs flaring, hissing threats.

Harry won't keep them off the guy for long, not when he's between them and their nests.

"Cover me," hisses Josh. And he's off, sprinting across the nesting ground. A raptor's muscles bunch to spring—I shoot it. Another moves towards Josh's temptingly moving form—and drops as Harry fires.

Josh has the city-guy's good arm over his shoulder already, and he's drag-carrying him back towards me. I shoot another raptor—so does Harry. The six survivors shrink back against the cliff sides, seeking shelter from the rifles now all the intruders are moving away from the nests.

"Let's move," hisses Josh as he staggers past me. The city-idiot's slumped full against him, barely helping himself along at all.

I back after them as fast as I can, keeping my rifle up, every muscle tense as my eyes strain for a glimpse of movement.

Nothing but silent stillness…

"Stay sharp," pants Josh. "They're gonna be mad as

heck." The tension in his voice is thick enough to slice granite. We've no cover from Harry, now. It's just me.

Still no raptors. How long until we reach the place we climbed down? How are we gonna get the suit back up that mountainside to Harry? Can Josh carry him outright? I can't help or we'll have no cover at all…

A faint scuff from behind me, ahead of Josh—I spin around just as Josh lets suit-guy fall, trying to bring his rifle up. I get off a shot a split second before the raptor carries Josh to the ground. I must've hit it because it screeches and thrashes until I put another bullet in its head. Its struggles have left Josh almost—but not quite—free from its weight, half-pinned against the cliffside.

I rush to him. "Josh!"

"I'm fine," he gasps. "Fine. Just concentrate…"

I drop to one knee with the cliff at my back, rifle ready, as suit-man groans and sobs on the other side of the dead raptor. "Come on, Josh!" I urge. "Get out from under there."

He's not wrenching around much or trying hard, that I can hear.

"Let me…catch my breath," he pants. "Listen a moment…speed is our…only chance. You get up and…run…straight back to…Harry. 'Kay?"

"What? You need me to cover you!"

"We'll be…right behind you… Get ready to…to run…"

I open my mouth to tell him again how stupid this plan is, but a movement further down the ravine snaps it closed *again. I watch, every muscle taut, but the raptor doesn't show itself again. Fine.*

"Come on, Josh. Grab the guy and let's move."

No answer. "Josh?"

I risk a glance. His eyes are oddly fixed. Staring blankly. I twist around. "Josh?" I grip his shoulder but his head just lolls forward, like a rag doll's. "JOSH!"

No response. I push the raptor's trailing wing-arm clear of Josh's stomach and bile surges up, choking me. His belly's slashed open, so much blood…

"Josh," I moan, my arm going around his shoulders, my hand cupping his cheek, but his eyes just look through me. "Why didn't you…why didn't you tell me?"

I could've helped you…

No, you couldn't, *says his unseeing gaze.* You would only have been distract—

Movement at the corner of my vision. I start to turn, fumbling to free my arms, grab my rifle—

I sit bolt up in my city-bunk, heart pounding, drenched in sweat. Ugh. What a horrible nightmare. All the worse for being so darn *plausible*. As dreams go, anyway. Neon markings, yeah right. And Josh would never have put Harry and me in that situation. But we did have a stressful time with some raptors in exactly that location, once, as an—eventual—consequence of helping some city-idiots. Well, Josh and I did. Harry was safe in the 'Vi, of course.

But I can't think about that now. I'm shaking, great shudders from head to toe, and my throat is so tight I can hardly breathe. I'm so scared the dream is true—in the only way that matters.

Because the police *still* haven't come to interview me. And I can only think of one reason for that.

Josh must be dead.

HARRY

This morning—Wednesday—I put on my fatigues and outdoor jacket, leaving the city-clothes over the back of the chair. I choose the pants and top that are in best condition, but there sure ain't any mistaking them for city-wear, Tat or Tidy.

When I come downstairs, Susannah stares at me for a long time, her mouth half-open to speak. But, in the end, she just asks me what I'd like for breakfast and doesn't mention my clothes.

Everyone stares at school, too. I fix a tough look on my face and stride along like I don't care. I'm not a city-boy, and I ain't gonna pretend to be.

DARRYL

Josh is dead.

The thought hammers through my mind all day.

However hard I try to dismiss the dream as just some stupid nightmare caused by the stress of our capture and forced relocation, it's transformed my fear, my mere suspicion, to a near-certainty that I can't shake off.

After all, why else wouldn't they question me? He must have died, alone and afraid, in some hospital bed. In the ambulance, maybe, before we even reached the city... Oh, if he *had* to die, why couldn't it have been in the 'Vi, his home? He was so peaceful after Father Ben's conditional baptism and we were there with him, Harry and Father Ben and me... Why couldn't he have died then, before the city-folk arrived?

But why did he have to die at all? It's the kidnappers' fault. We'd never have gone *near* Jason's illegal rex farm if it wasn't for them, and Josh wouldn't have gotten bitten!

I wish they would fall into a rex pen *full* of juvenile rex. I wish— With effort, I rein in my vengeful thoughts. The homily yesterday was all about loving our enemies. I can't let myself think like this.

I want Dad, Uncle Z, Darryl, Harry... Josh whispered. So desperate to be sure he was properly baptized, so he could be with everyone he cared about, forever. If I've got to wait a lifetime to see him again, that really, really stinks. But the least I can do is make sure I don't let him down. I don't want to let Dad down, either, because the same goes for him, now, doesn't it?

Okay, Lord. I don't want them to fall into a rex pen. I want them locked up in prison and visited by Fernanda Matthews until they repent and throw themselves on your mercy. Yeah, make them repent, Lord. Make them!

That's about the worst acceptable thing I can think of to wish on them.

HARRY

"So, have you ever killed anything?" After several days staring and giving me a wide berth, a few boys from my home room have settled—cautiously—at the same lunch table with me.

My turn to stare at him. What sort of stupid question is that? "Sure."

They stare back as though I've said something amazing.

"What's it like?"

"Like?"

"Is it...exciting?"

"Scary?" asks another boy.

"Does it make you puke?" asks yet another.

"Puke? Why would it? It just depends." I shrug. "If someone is in danger, it can be scary, but there's a heck of a rush of relief if you get it before it gets one of you. If it's just routine hunting, it can be boring as anything. If you're hunting your dinner, that can be satisfying, y'know? If you're culling something injured or sick, you can feel real good you've put it out of its misery. If it's a really difficult shot and you hit it, that's a great feeling."

"How old were you when you first killed something?" asks another boy, hot-eyed.

"Urm?" Why are they obsessed with this? "I dunno. I guess by the time I was eleven it was normal for Dad to send me out with a .22—uh, that's a type of rifle—to pop off a few rabbits for dinner. Probably shot my first rabbit at about seven. Maybe six."

The boys stare at me with awe-filled eyes, as though one of the characters in the games they play incessantly on their communicators and talk about non-stop has just sat down amongst them.

I shrug, uncomfortable. "It really ain't a big deal." I keep coming out with hunter-speak, these days. I guess it's a tiny defiance that makes me feel closer to poor Josh, wherever he is. Darryl was doing it too, when I saw her on Sunday.

But they go right on staring. At least when they're pestering me with silly questions they're not on their communicators, looking at those *pictures*. They're *always* looking at them. Offering me a look...

How much longer can I avoid it?

DARRYL

Fei and Marnie dash straight up the stairs when we get back from school on Wednesday—something about some new nail polish—while Kerri follows at a dignified saunter, but I head for Ms. Williamson's room. She's not there. I'm standing in the hall, looking around, reluctant to go upstairs without asking about Josh—*he's dead, whispers that little voice*—when Ms. Williamson appears from the parlor.

"Ah, Darryl, I hoped that might be you. There are some people here to see you."

She ushers me toward the parlor. People? Harry? Mau?

But when I step inside, two policewomen are sitting at the table, one dark-skinned, one fair-skinned, both grave-faced. My heart seizes up in my chest. Why are they here? To interview me?

...Or to tell me he's dead?

I stand, staring at them, unable to move.

"Darryl Franklyn?" the black cop—slightly older and more senior?—smiles at me. "Is it okay if we call you Darryl?"

"*Is he alive?*" My voice strangles itself.

They look surprised. "Who?"

"*Josh.* Is he *alive?*"

"Joshua Wilson? Yes, yes, he's alive. It was touch and go, but he's out of ICU now and— Oh, are you...are you okay?"

The relief strikes me like a physical blow, stripping all my control away. I collapse into the other chair, sobbing so hard it feels like I'm going to tear apart. I sense Ms. Williamson move alongside me; her hand grips my shoulder, squeezing slightly. I want to get myself together but I can't. I haven't lost it this badly for *years*.

"Her case worker refused to tell her if the young man was okay," murmurs Ms. Williamson, when the policewomen carry on exclaiming in dismay and confusion.

"That seems needlessly cruel!" Indignation fills the white cop's voice.

"I make no comment." Ms. Williamson rubs my shoulder a few more times. "I will go and make everyone a cup of coffee. I must ask you to give Darryl a few minutes to get herself together."

"Of course."

"Naturally."

To my embarrassment, once Ms. Williamson has gone, the policewomen take it upon themselves to rub my back and pat my shoulder, murmuring soothing things. City-folk can be nice, even if they are wet as lettuce. Though I guess city-cops can't be totally limp if they deal with the thugs that prowl the city streets.

"I thought he was *dead*," I sniff, when I finally get

control of my voice back. "No one came to interview me, so I thought—"

"Not in the least," says the black cop—Officer Peterson, a watery glance at her uniform reveals. "Whatever the doctors have said to state prosecution, they clearly feel it's now worth assembling the case against him, so he must be out of danger."

"Yep, he's strong, that one," says the white cop—Officer Werren. "Well, his body is. It sounds like he has some psychological iss—" She breaks off and clears her throat, patting my shoulder some more.

Psychological issues. I bet. Poor Josh. Is he still freaking out? Will he be able to get used to being in-city at all, or is it just going to be unending torment for him?

There's only one thing I can do to help.

Once Ms. Williamson has brought us all coffee— mine full of sugar—and we've made harmless chit-chat while drinking it and I've wiped my face and eaten a cookie and stopped shaking, the policewomen get out their hand-pads and put their professional faces back on. Ms. Williamson sits down quietly in the corner— guess she's the chaperone.

"Darryl, could you tell us about the events that led to you and your brother leaving your family farm in Joshua Wilson's habitat vehicle last spring?"

How very non-leading of them. Waiting to see what I say, who I blame.

I blame the kidnappers. And Fernanda.

I tell them everything. Well, not quite everything. I don't mention West, Thiago, or Ed. I leave them to assume that our fuel tanks and ammo boxes magically refilled themselves all year. Which they'll know ain't true, but they're not hearing it from me.

I don't say a word about seeing Father Ben those other times, either, or the midwinter fair. Okay, I don't mention Jason, either. I'll leave it to Josh whether he wants to up Jason's thirst for vengeance to that degree.

But I tell them everything else.

It's all I can do for Josh, now.

HARRY

"Harry, could you tell us about the events that led to you and your sister leaving your family farm in Joshua Wilson's habitat vehicle last spring?"

The police have finally come. They say Josh is alive. I'm shaking with relief. I could hardly breathe until they told me. But now they want to know everything.

I'm a little kid again, running across the farmyard to Dad; he swings me up into the air, I'm laughing...

But Josh... Even the thought of prison gave him a full-blown panic attack. He's suffering because he helped us. And Father Ben, too...

The cop cuffs Father Ben's wrists, spins him around,

pushing him against the wall as he searches him...

...Josh is screaming, begging, trying to struggle, but he's too weak...

Almost a year with no ransom demand. Darryl's right. We have to assume Dad's dead.

"I'm sorry, Dad," I whisper.

"What was that, son?" asks one of the policemen.

"Nothing."

I don't tell them about West, Thiago, or Ed, or anything extra about Father Ben. I don't dare mention Jason, either.

But I tell them everything else.

DARRYL

It's not just the one interview, of course. There are several. A couple with psychologists or therapists. The worst thing is the doctor's examination, but I would have insisted on that, because I know out of it all, it's the thing that will help Josh the most.

I can tell the difference in the detectives' attitudes, afterward. Even Ms. Williamson, who hasn't seemed inclined to assume the worst about Josh quite the way Fernanda does, seems to think better of him now.

There doesn't seem to be much hope that he won't go to prison. But he seems likely to get a light sentence. He's not well enough to be put on trial yet, apparently. I ask if I can see him, but that's a hard no from the police and above all from Fernanda. The doctor's report doesn't make any difference with *her*. I'm not sure if she doesn't really believe it or if she just thinks living in a HabVi all that time was such unimaginable trauma I'll be lucky to ever recover from it, regardless of anything else.

I still have to see the counselor twice a week, anyway, which is so tedious. I try to focus the conversations on my move in-city, since that's my biggest 'trauma,' and if that doesn't work I shift the conversations onto Dad, 'cause that was a huge deal, sure enough—even if it didn't totally wrench my entire world apart quite the way this has done.

HARRY

"How can you say your father's death—or kidnapping, whichever it was—was less traumatic than simply moving to the city?" asks the counselor, several weeks later. It's a more leading question than she usually asks, but I guess she's getting frustrated that she can't understand my point of view.

How do I explain it? Like Fernanda, she's so convinced that city-life is the only life suitable for anyone, especially anyone under the age of eighteen. Actually, I've had an image in my mind for weeks, now, as everyone smiles at me and pats my head and tells me I'm safe now and isn't my life so good? I've never tried to share it with anyone, though.

"Say my life is a piece of woven fabric..." I sure hope this is gonna make sense. "And Dad is a really bright, wonderful, important strand that's crucial to the pattern. Yank that thread out—that's losing Dad. The pattern will never be completely right, ever again. But the piece of fabric is still *there*. Coming in-city—that's like *my* strand is yanked out of the piece of fabric and someone is trying to force it into another weave, glue it in, make it stay any way they can. But it doesn't belong there, so it's always gonna look wrong. Feel wrong. Does *that* make any sense?"

The counselor frowns and doodles with her stylus for a moment, clearly playing for time. Susannah, who, with my agreement, is allowed to sit quietly in the corner during the sessions, looks unsettled. Good. I wanted her in here to begin with because I felt so awkward with the counselor, but if it's actually teaching her something about how country-folk think...

Good.

Not that it should matter, soon. Uncle Mau has a date for a custody hearing. Not for almost two months, but it should be an open and shut case. I mean, Uncle Mau was our guardian before Dad married Carol, he has all the old paperwork, and there are even messages between Dad and Uncle Mau making it clear Dad was about to get everything straight. There can't be any doubt about Dad's intentions. The judge needs a really serious reason not to honor that, right?

DARRYL

Josh, I really hope you're okay, or as okay as you can be. I can't say Harry or I like city-life much, but we're well, so please don't worry about us. Maurice may get custody in only two more months. We told the police all about Dad so things will go as easily as possible for you. I'm praying for you every day, and I'm so sorry you're in this mess because of us. Thank you for trying so hard to help us find Dad. I don't know how often I can communicate with you because Fernanda thinks you're evil incarnate, despite the evidence.
Please be well, we miss you so much.
Love, Darryl

I put the lid on the pen and wait to be sure the ink has dried on the piece of paper. I still don't know where Josh is, but I have a plan.

Okay, it's dry. I fold it carefully. On the front half

I've drawn the nicest Easter cross, decorated with flowers, that I could while sitting here on the closed toilet seat using a book balanced on my knees as a desk. It's a much flimsier Easter card than the normal one I now slip it inside, but I don't want it to be obvious there are two in the envelope.

It's Easter Sunday tomorrow and I've made very sure to chat to Father Gayle after each of the three Easter week services. I'd already spoken to him after Sunday Masses, of course—Ms. Williamson is even allowing me to attend church unaccompanied, now. He seems friendly, so I'm gonna ask him to send the card to Father Ben, who's still being held in prison, can you believe?

"Seriously?" Incredulity filled my voice after Ms. Williamson told me. Apparently she's allowed to speak more freely about Father Ben, though she's not actually allowed to tell me where he is.

"It's the Wickmore Amendment. No bail for anyone awaiting trial in any crime involving hunters. You must know that hunters let out on bail rarely end up in court; they vanish into the wilds and leave state."

"Father Ben ain't a hunter, though."

"But Mr. Wilson is—unluckily for your priest friend."

Since Father Ben's 'crime' hinges on Josh's, he can't be tried first. Poor Father Ben. I hope he's okay. But I also hope Father Ben can pass the second card on to Josh. He probably knows where he is.

A worm of disquiet wriggles in my belly. Should I be trying to get him to do that? Haven't I got him in enough trouble?

I still haven't made up my mind when I reach the church the following morning, though I've got the card with me, tucked in my big jacket pocket. I struggle to concentrate on the Mass, to not be distracted, but it's hard. Afterward, I kneel for a while and pray, enjoying a few minutes peace and quiet, or trying to—my mind keeps circling. Should I give Father Gayle the card?

Mr. Jefford has brought Harry to church again and is now drifting around admiring the building the way he usually does while waiting after Mass. Mr. and Mrs. Jefford have invited me to have Easter lunch with them, too, and Ms. Williamson is allowing me to go over there for the first time. Will Father Gayle tell Ms. Williamson about the card? Will he tell Fernanda? I don't want to harm Mau's chances of getting custody of us.

But Josh is sick and all alone. Are they refusing to tell him anything about us, the way they are us about him?

Finally, I get to my feet. Father Gayle is bidding goodbye to the last few people. This is my chance to speak to him.

"Keep Mr. Jefford away for a few minutes, would

you?" I ask Harry, pulling the card far enough out that he can read the name on it.

Harry's eyes brighten and he nods eagerly, genuflecting and bounding off. I move quickly to Father Gayle as the couple he's speaking to leave.

"Hi, Darryl. Nice to see you here again this morning." I must look puzzled, because he adds, "Since you were at the Vigil last night. Not everyone comes to both."

"Oh. Well, I wouldn't miss it. We're lucky to have one single Mass during the two weeks around Easter, out in the country, y'know."

"So you're liking the city?" He sounds so hopeful.

I shake my head. "No, really not. Just the Masses."

He sighs. "Well, it's early days."

I try not to scowl at him. It's Easter Sunday *and* I'm about to ask him for a favor! Am I? Yeah. I've simply *got* to get *something* to Josh, even if just the once.

"Father Gayle, do you know Father Ben, my parish priest?"

"My brother-priest who's languishing in jail right now thanks to your shenanigans?" Father Gayle sounds more rueful than accusing. "Sure, I know him a little."

"He didn't do anything wrong. Anyway, um, I got an Easter card for him. But my social worker won't tell me where he is so I was just wondering if you could send it for me?" I hold it out.

He takes it reluctantly. "An Easter card?"

"Yeah. I didn't seal it yet. You can look if you like."
That was the compromise I made with myself, 'cause I
do feel bad even slightly tricking a priest.

He glances at the back of the envelope but doesn't
actually open it in front of me. "I'll drop it in to him myself. I guess he'd welcome a visit from a friendly face."

HARRY

*The icy winter wind howls around the turret and I hunch
into my coat. I'd rather be below but it's Darryl's turn to
deep-clean the living area floor so Josh and I have to stay up
here in chilly exile for a while longer.*

*"Josh?" The hatch is closed to keep the heat in down
below, so it's a good chance to ask him about something
that...that keeps creeping into my mind more and more.*

"Yeah?"

"Um, have you ever seen, like...um. Pictures?*"*

*A stillness falls over him, but he simply says,
"Pictures?"*

Heck, is he gonna make me say it?

"Girls?"

*"Yeah." His tone is very level. "I have. When I were
about your age, a guy slipped me a physical copy of a
magazine in the 'Vi-park one time. And I looked at it."*

His tone sure isn't encouraging and my cheeks go red

hot. I thought Josh was a safe person to ask, but I can sense his disapproval. I might as well have asked Dad or Father Ben! "So, uh... what happened to it?"

"You really wanna know?" He raises one eyebrow, challenging.

I nod, though I'm starting to doubt if I do.

"My dad caught me with it. I got uppity and told him there were nothing wrong with it, the women chose to do it and got paid well—that was what the guy had told me. So Dad said that were good news, we needed a new winch and it's an expensive bit of kit, but we could get the money real quick if I just took my clothes off and we sold some photos online."

I can feel my eyes bulging. "What? What did you do?"

"Shut myself in my berth and cried and refused to come out."

"And what did your dad do?"

"Well, he and Uncle Z turned me on the spit for a while. Kept knocking on my door, real serious, telling me to come out at once so we could get our new winch, since I thought it were okay, until finally I yelled that I didn't think it were okay, it were horrible and wrong and I weren't never gonna do it and no one else should have to neither! At which point they said good, they also thought it were horrible and wrong and they were glad I now understood that too. So I came down and got a hug and chucked the magazine in the incinerator. So that's what happened to it. Ash. Never looked *at pictures again."*

He eyes me, making me want to squirm in my seat. "I'm kinda surprised you think that kinda thing is okay, though."

"I-I didn't say I thought it was okay…" I stutter. "I was just…just curious…"

"Yeah? Would you be happy some guy were looking at Darryl because he were just curious?" His eyes glint ominously.

"Okay, okay!" Heck, I could cook raw meat on my cheeks. "I get it! It's wrong. I agree. Okay?"

Josh's smile makes me feel even more of a shame-faced kid…

I open my eyes to a white, white room with lime green edging. The city. I sure wish I was back in the 'Vi, even with Josh turning me on the spit like that. I just wish…I just wish I was back there, period. Susannah and Philip made sure I saw plenty of Darryl this Easter break, but summer semester starts tomorrow. Back to seeing her only once a week. Back to weird, boring school. Back to those city-boys with their communicators.

No wonder I had that dream.

DARRYL

Nerves churn my stomach as I approach Father Gayle the following Sunday.

"Hi, Father."

"Hi, Darryl." Is it me or is he eyeing me closely? "Well, I delivered your card. Or should I say *cards*?"

I try to look more apologetic than guilty. "Will Father Ben send it on?"

"I thought it best not to ask." Father Gayle sounds grim. "I do try to maintain a good relationship with the home, you know? And this case hasn't come to trial yet. Don't think I'll be your go-between."

"I don't," I say quickly. "It was just a one-off."

"I read the note, so I believe you." But he looks at me and sighs and shakes his head. Whatever Father Ben told him wasn't enough. Well, once Josh is tried and gets the lightest possible sentence—please God!— everyone will know he didn't do anything wrong!

When will that be, though? Surely he's well on the way to recovering, now? I suppose it takes time for the prosecution to put a case together. Though considering how long we were missing, you'd think they'd have most of it prepared already.

HARRY

"Get a load of this, Harry!" Yates shoves his communicator in my face, grinning. "Are hunter-girls this hot?"

I push his hand away, trying not to look at the

screen, though part of me really wants to. "I'm busy."

"Busy? You're only *reading*! Look what you're missing!"

"No, thanks."

"You always act so weird when we get out the pics. Why don't you want to look?"

Aw, *outage*! Everyone in my home room is staring at me, now, and I'm frozen like a mammal in the headlights.

I can look.

I can make an excuse.

Or I can...

I swallow. This lot think I'm all tough and cool. What will they think if I—

"Well? What's your problem?"

Josh may not even be in this *city*, but I can almost feel his gaze on me.

I raise my head, jut out my jaw, and fix a tough sneer on my face. "*I'm* not the one with a problem. Hunters don't look at that crap." Okay, I'm sure some do, but they wouldn't admit it to the Elders, so it counts as 'something hunters don't do.'

Confusion, not derision, covers their faces.

"What's wrong with it?"

"It's totally *normal*."

"Why is it a problem for hunters?"

My brows scrunch together in confusion of my

own. "Don't you have *sisters*? Would you be happy if they were in those photos? If *you* had to be?"

Indifferent shrugs. "If I *chose* to."

"Well, *my* sister wouldn't, so who cares."

"Mine's too *ugly*!"

They fall around laughing and I just stare, unable to find any words. They don't even *understand* why I've got a problem with it? Why a lot of farmers and hunters would?

I am *never* going to feel at home here.

And I'm not sure I even want to.

DARRYL

Another month crawls by, April turning slowly into May. I become better at excusing myself to enjoy the company of a book on my handPad when Marnie and Fei get their cosmetics out, but books can only brighten up my life so much. Ms. Williamson gives me permission to go out for walks, but the city air is smoggy and clogs my lungs. Virtually no animals, just dogs. And you get funny looks if you walk up to some stranger's dog and start giving it some attention. Dog-theft is a big thing, Kerri explains.

The only other animals are pigeons and the occasional hawk that preys on them—and rats. Lots of those. Grey furry ones that scurry along gutters and lean, hungry-eyed two-legged ones that scuttle into alleyways—and, presumably, steal dogs, among other things. Sometimes I wish I still had my rifle or my hunting knife—but they're safe in the 'Vi.

I hope.

HARRY

I sit at my perfect white desk in my perfect white room, trying to concentrate. The homework assignment is actually really easy: what I want to be when I grow up. It's just that thinking about it keeps taking my mind far away from here—and tying my stomach in an aching knot. But I've got to do something. I can't just sit here thinking about life on the farm. However much I want to.

Or life in the 'Vi…

Snow billows past the turret window, roiling whiteness.

"I thought you said no fresh snow today?" I remark.

The slight lift of Josh's eyebrow says he recognizes a subject change when he hears one, but he goes along with it. I guess he's said what he wanted to say about 'pictures.'

"It ain't snowing," he says dryly. "That's just the wind picking up the drifts and flinging 'em around."

"Oh." I peer out, shaking my head. "Heck, it's wild up here in the mountains."

"Yeah, too cold, too exposed, and the wildlife is hungry,

super-dangerous. Sane hunters never over-winter at this kinda altitude. Unless they're wanted men, anyway." Like us.

Although Josh usually endures the freezing temperatures without comment, he sounds a little glum — though about the weather or the wantedness, who knows.

Darryl's voice comes over the intercom. "It's all clean and dry now. Come down whenever you want."

Whenever I want? Er, that would be half an hour ago, thanks, sis!

I try to restrain my headlong dive for the hatch to a fractionally more dignified surge. A slight smile darts over Josh's face, regardless. But then his head comes up sharply and he goes motionless. Listening. I stay very still as well.

Danger?

Josh reaches out and yanks the lever to raise the windows on the side away from the wind. Snow and icy gusts still blast us as the glass rises, but he ignores it.

Another moment of keen listening and disbelief wrinkles Josh's brow.

"Heck, it is an engine!" he breathes, leaning to lift the hatch and call, "Darryl, get up the turret with your rifle." He slides down the ladder, adding, "Someone's in trouble!"

An eddy of wind finally brings the sound to my ears. Frantic revving. Honking. And…

A chill goes down my spine.

From the warbling cries and ominous thuds, some very

irate pachysaurs are smashing up something metal—with the extreme prejudice only an irate pachy can bring to bear.

A car door slamming out in the street jerks my mind back to the city. Oh yeah. Homework. I'm supposed to be doing my homework...

DARRYL

A couple of days into May, I finally come in from school one day and there's a physical newspaper lying casually on the table in the hall. Where there isn't usually. I snatch it up and turn the pages quickly, scanning the headlines. Nothing. Nothing. More nothing. Maybe Ms. Williamson didn't 'accidentally' leave it here for me aftera...

There!

HUNTER AND PRIEST SENTENCED IN KIDNAPPING CASE.

I scan the short article, my eyes flying over the words. Josh was found guilty of felony kidnapping only, thank God! Court satisfied there was no ill intent and no bad conduct...sentence...*twelve months with possibility of parole after nine months.*

A *year*? In-city? Oh, poor Josh!

And Father Ben? Found guilty of concealing the

whereabouts of minors from the authorities...satisfied no ill intent...no bad conduct...sentence...five months, possibility of parole after three. Well, he's done two already, so maybe they'll let him out in only another month. That's something, though bad enough considering we totally dragged him into it. But Josh...

Poor Josh. I guess it *is* the lightest possible sentence, but... Will he be okay?

HARRY

"What did you put?" asks Yates, when I sit beside him for our Personal Development class.

"Farmer." I got the assignment done eventually.

"Really?"

"Sure."

"Thought you were a hunter?"

"Farmer first. Then a hunter. That's my order of career preference, too."

"Isn't farming just, like, boring and dangerous? Living out there? Predators. Nothing to do?"

I shrug. "I actually used to dream of being all kinds of things. Pilot. Bullet train driver. SPARKie. But when our stepmom said we had to leave the farm and go in-city—I knew. Didn't, kinda, put it right into words in my head that very moment, but looking back, that was when I knew. I want to be a farmer. I figured it out properly while I was off hunting. But now I'm stuck in here."

Yates eyes me sideways. "You really feel *stuck*? Really want to go back out there?"

"Yep."

"Huh." He shakes his head, then brightens, tapping his handPad. "I want to be a famous presenter. I did a local interview for the school last year, you know? I can send you the link..."

I attempt to look vaguely interested. Over three more years of *this*? My heart sinks like lead.

Uncle Mau *has* to get custody. He simply has to!

DARRYL

There was no picture with the news article. I'm glad the press aren't all over the story, really, but...a picture would've been nice. I still don't have one.

A truck revs loudly, trying to inch through solid traffic. I hunch my shoulders and walk on, my mind drifting…

The 'Vi lurches forward almost as soon as Josh reaches the cab. I've already hauled myself into the turret and shut the hatch to prevent Harry or myself falling down it. Snow spins up from under the wheels as Josh gets us underway, cutting the visibility down to almost nothing.

Despite the icy gale rushing through the turret I don't

move to close the windows and nor does Harry. We both listen, trying to pinpoint where the noise is coming from. Heck, I hope Josh could tell because…

"The wind's throwing the sound all over the place," I mutter.

"Josh was looking that way." Harry points along the mountainside in the direction Josh is probably trying to take us, though we're weaving around all over the slope as Josh hunts for bare rock—or at least smaller drifts—that won't bog the huge vehicle down. Even with the winter tracks fitted around our wheels we're chancing it, moving around in this.

"I think he's right," I say, as another flurry of snow and revving and mean-sounding warbling hits our ears.

"Remember," Josh's voice comes over the intercom, "if you have to fire, aim for the neck and chest. Not the head unless you're sure of an eye shot."

"Yeah, yeah—" Harry breaks off as a horrible thud-crunch-tinkle gusts through the air.

"Well, that sounded final." I take over the intercom button from Harry. "Josh, I think our mystery vehicle just crashed."

"I'm going as fast as I can," is all Josh says. "Be ready."

I hook a pair of snow goggles from under the console and thrust them at Harry, slipping into a pair myself, then raising my rifle. With these on, there's just a chance we might be able to see to actually hit something…

Here's the alley. With a quick glance to check no one's paying close attention to me, I crouch and drop the dog biscuit into the empty take-out carton I've been using as a bowl. Withdrawing a little way, I don't have long to wait. The rodo is already creeping out to get his daily treat—and giving me mine.

HARRY

"What are they doing over there?" I stare across the playground, to where a group of older boys are gathered around, gawking at something on the ground, whooping and cheering.

"Better not to ask," says Yates. "Hey, you know the city channel is looking for a 'teen voice'? They'll have, like, five thousand applicants, but still. I'm going to go for it."

"Great," I say, still distracted by whatever those older boys are up to. The ones inside the circle...I glimpse sticks poking at something. "Good luck."

"You could apply too, I guess. You really should start your own Net channel: A Hunter-kid in the City or something like that."

"Yeah, maybe not."

Yates shrugs. He's mentioned interviewing me on his own channel several times. Does he really like me, or am I just a possible asset?

"Yo, suit yourself. Less competition for me. I need to raise my game if I'm going to be the new Teen Voice. Maybe Dad will buy me a new vidcam—"

A brief lull in playground noise carries a tiny frantic squeaking to my ears. Coming from...

Leaving Yates in mid-sentence, I dash across and shoulder my way through the bigger boys. What...? There's a little mouse in the center of the circle and they're poking and prodding it with their sticks, laughing as it stumbles weakly this way and that, trying to escape.

"*You*—" Angrier than I ever remember being, I shove right into the middle of the group and put the poor creature out of its misery with one solid blow from my heavy hunter boot.

"You vicious animals!" The words finally come as they stare at me, looking as shocked as I feel, though maybe for a different reason. "You want to kill a mouse, *kill it*, don't *torture it* like that!"

As I push my way out of the circle and march off, one of them finally finds his tongue.

"That was *my* mouse, filthy hunter dog! You'll pay for that!"

Maybe not the time to point out that hunters are far more like cats. I keep walking.

DARRYL

"So you don't like him?" Kerri challenges.

Other than explaining some city-stuff to me, most of my conversations with girls from the home revolve around rural lifestyles—a source of fascination to them—or Josh. It's as hard to convince them that Josh and I aren't an item as it is everyone else.

"Of course I *like* him. He's...he's like family."

"You mean, he feels like a *brother*?"

I hesitate. Josh definitely feels like *family*, that I'm sure of. Part of *my* family. But I'd be lying if I said he felt like my *brother*, exactly. Not like Harry.

"Josh is...Josh is *Josh*, okay?"

"What does that even *mean*, Darryl?"

I can't answer, because I don't know myself. I just know I miss him so bad it keeps me awake at night.

HARRY

I lob a stone onto the water and watch it bounce three times before disappearing. I only learned to skim stones this last year. Josh taught me while Darryl kept watch, beside huge, still lakes that sometimes reflected the mountains like a mirror on a calm day. I don't get all lyrical about nature quite the way Darryl and Josh do, but those big lakes were awe-inspiring. Lakes weren't really something Darryl and I had ever seen, except a glimpse in the distance while driving somewhere on a road. The city-folk call *this* a 'lake.'

"Puddle," I say.

Darryl glances at me. "Huh?"

"Exception City 'lake.' More of a puddle, right?"

"Pond, maybe."

The city-folk jog and stroll around the graveled tracks of the 'country-park,' apparently satisfied with this tiny artificial patch of carefully landscaped greenery. Susannah and Philip have started bringing us here after Sunday lunch for a walk. They obviously think they're giving us a real treat, a real home away from home. The sad thing is, I do actually look forward to it, and I think Darryl does too. It's better than nothing.

"I found a spot where a rodento'saur lives while I was out running a while back," says Darryl, busy choosing a pebble of her own. "I've been giving it dog treats. But the other day some city-folk glimpsed it. Just flitting away down its alley—you know how shy those little things are. One of them *screamed*, can you believe? They were talking about an exterminator."

"What?" I stare at her incredulously. "Why? A few rodos are just what this places needs, eat up the rats. It's not like they're trying to breed rabbits, like on a farm." We never wanted rodento'saurs around, but farmers who don't bother with rabbits always like to have a couple to eat the mammalian rodents.

Darryl shrugs, her lips pulling down sourly. "It's just 'cause it's a 'saur, I guess. This whole place is about pretending 'saurs don't really exist, except for in the zoo. Wish I could catch it and keep it to tame, but now I don't even dare feed it anymore. Better if it stays as shy as possible. In case the exterminator wasn't just talk."

"You could give it to me!"

Darryl smiles. "Yeah, maybe." From her tone, if she did catch it she'd have a hard time parting with it.

"You think Josh can toe the line enough to be out in nine months?" It ain't the first time I've said it, but I can't help coming back to it. Less than six months, now, technically, since he's nearing the end of his third month of imprisonment if you count the pre-trial time.

"I hope so, but who knows? I guess it depends if they believe that he can't help it if he has a panic attack or if they just see it as acting up."

She lobs her stone. It skips only twice and sinks. Something I'm better at. Or maybe her heart isn't in it. Josh taught her, too, while I kept watch. I stare out over the small body of water, trying to keep my mind on majestic mountain lakes.

"Harry? What's the matter?"

"Huh?" Uh-oh. "Nothing."

"Tell me about 'nothing' then."

"It's really not a big deal."

"Then it doesn't matter you telling me."

Darn. There's no keeping secrets from my big sis. She's gonna keep weaseling until she gets it out of me—or she's gonna worry all week if she doesn't. "Fine, it's just school. There's this group of older boys..." I tell her what happened with the mouse. "And now they've started watching me, like they want to be able to say they got revenge on a hunter and lived to tell the tale. I'm just ignoring them, walking tall and looking tough, like I've got six uncles West's size, all with Thiago's temper, who'll gut them in their sleep if they lay a finger on me. I'm really not sure how long that's gonna hold them off, is all. Apparently the one guy—I think of him as Allosaur, big and dumb—he bought the poor mouse in a pet store and they meant to 'play with it' over and over, so they're super cheesed off."

I shake my head, trying to dismiss the issue. "Anyway, if Uncle Mau gets custody next month, we'll be outta here."

"Let's hope so—problem solved."

Yeah, in a month we'll be packing our bags and getting into Uncle Mau's truck and bye-bye city, right?

DARRYL

Harry's quiet as Philip and Susannah Jefford drive me back to the home. Is he thinking about the custody hearing? Everything ought to be okay after that, I know it should. But...I can't help remembering Fernanda's reaction to the possibility of Mau's guardianship, back when she first showed up at the farm. What if the judge thinks the same way? On the other hand, it's one thing to disapprove of a chosen guardian and quite another to actually go against a parent's clearly expressed wish without some very serious reason, surely?

"Well, here we are," says Susannah, as Philip turns the corner to the street where the home is squeezed between a block of modern offices and another grand old terraced house. "I hope you have a good week at school, Darryl."

I open my mouth to reply, but Harry grabs my arm. "Hey, look!"

My eyes focus on the battered truck sitting by the curb, and I'm opening my door almost before we've pulled to a halt.

Harry's right behind me as I rush up to the truck's window. "Sandra! Riley! Fred!"

"Darryl, Harry, there you are!"

They're out of the truck almost as fast. Sandra wraps us both in big hugs, Riley in more restrained ones.

Fred, a year older than Harry, lurks with his hands shoved in his pockets, grinning awkwardly. "Yo, you two, how've you been?"

"Everything was fine until a couple of months ago,"

Harry replies. "Except for Dad. Since then it's just been concrete and stink." He kicks the curb irritably.

"Aw, you poor things." Sandra hugs me again. "We were going to come see you at Easter, but we didn't have an address. Maurice finally got it out of them and there was no Mass today so we thought we'd come along."

Yeah, rural priests are scarce and ours is in jail because of us. How many Masses are they getting these days? But Philip and Susannah come over before I can say anything and by the time introductions have been made, Ms. Williamson is standing in the front doorway, looking down the steps at us.

"Friends of yours, Darryl?"

"Our closest neighbors." I eye her warily. Will she send them away? "They drove three hours to get here."

"Darryl's not allowed unsupervised non-family visits yet" —Ms. Williamson looks over my shoulder to Riley and Sandra—"but you can see her in the parlor."

Phew!

With three Wahlburgs, two Jeffords, two Franklyns, and Ms. Williamson the parlor is packed. Riley, Sandra, Fred, Harry, and I cluster around the table, while Philip, Susannah, and Ms. Williamson sit around the walls.

Riley shoots the chaperones an uncomfortable look, like he's not sure if he's supposed to ignore them or include them, then opens his bag and places a cardboard box on the table. From it he produces two farm-style little Easter baskets, pushing one in front of Harry and one in front of me.

"Sorry they're so late." He grins. "We didn't get them to Mau in time before Easter."

Mau brought us each a typical Carr Easter basket—expensive chocolate bunnies and shop-bought candy—when he was in-city just before Easter. These baskets from the Wahlburgs are more home-made, with eggs and little candy crosses instead of Mau's more secular stuff. I could tell Easter baskets from our neighbors apart at a glance, I've seen enough of them over the years.

"Thanks!" says Harry.

"Thank you," I say. "Uh...we didn't get anything for you guys..."

Even Fred shrugs this away. Sandra's taking a smaller wooden box from another bag. "A Ha—" She glances at the chaperones and swallows the rest as though unsure if it's a forbidden word. "Some guys stopped by just before Easter, asked if we'd be seeing you and left these."

A HabVi? Technicolor HabVi; West, Thiago, and Ed's 'Vi? Must be. I'm touched they thought of us, especially since they're no doubt trying to keep a low profile until they're sure the city-folk aren't out to punish whoever helped us evade capture all that time.

Easter is the biggest festival of the hunter year, though.

Harry and I work the lid off the box, me trying to be careful, Harry too impatient for my liking. But when we pull several handfuls of loose dried grass out, we find two intact eggs nestling underneath. Real eggs.

"Wow!"

Yeah, I second that! They're tall, narrow ornithomimous eggs, not huge like from an Edmo or something, but they've been beautifully painted, hunter-style, with patterns that I bet are all about Easter. There are little crosses and something that might represent an open tomb, among other things, in bright colors. I lift one out, and so does Harry.

"These are *heavy*." Harry checks underneath. "Hey, there's a little hole. I bet they're full of chocolate and fudge and who knows what, like Josh said."

Hunters inject all sorts of yummy fillings into their decorated eggs, apparently.

"It's *full* of chocolate?" says Fred, eyes widening. "But why make it so pretty? You'll have to break it to eat the insides."

Harry rolls his eyes slightly, making me grin because I can almost hear him thinking something about hunters and all their traditions. Fortunately, Josh told us all about hunter Easter eggs already. "Well," I say, "the idea is, you keep the egg from Easter until Pentecost, enjoying looking at it and appreciating the gift properly and practicing your self-control. Then you break it and eat it, reminding yourself of the impermanence of physical beauty and goods."

"Huh?" Fred veers between baffled and horrified. "Why does an Easter egg have to be so, uh...so...*heavy*?"

"Because it's full of chocolate and fudge," says Harry, straight-faced.

"Oh, ha-ha!" They have a shoving match with their forearms until I pull the eggs away to protect them. The beautifully painted shells could easily get cracked, even with the solid insides.

"So, uh, these are real *Technicolor* eggs, right?" I ask Riley and Sandra.

"Sure are." Riley winks, face turned away from our pesky chaperones. "I mean, look at all those *colors*."

HARRY

All too soon Ms. Williamson is saying she's sorry but the visit wasn't scheduled and there are things she needs to do, and Riley and Sandra and Fred are getting up to leave. Sandra hugs us both all over again, and I don't care that Fred is watching, I just hug her back, hard.

"I wish we could go with you," I say, blinking hard, because my eyes have gone all foggy.

"Aw, so do we, Harry, so do we. But Maurice will

be bringing you home in just weeks now, right?"

"I sure hope so."

"We'll have a cook-out on your birthday, Harry, to celebrate," says Riley. "Weather's getting good, now."

We wave them off, and soon I'm in the car with Philip and Susannah. They keep shooting each other worried looks as we drive. What's up? Do they think meeting other farmers might corrupt me, or something?

"Harry," says Philip, once we've sat down to dinner, "Mrs. Wahlburg mentioned the result of the custody case as though it was a foregone conclusion. You do know it's up to the judge, right?"

"Of course. But Dad's wishes were clear."

"Yes, but...if you'll forgive me mentioning a painful subject...that was *before* your stepmother—and possibly your father too—perished due to...to wildlife. That has to affect any decision concerning a suitable environment for you and your sister. They'll almost certainly consider that a city environment is now more appropriate, surely you realize that?"

I stare at him. He's just broken some carefully maintained dam in the back of my mind, releasing an ice-cold flood through my body. "Why? If I was a city-boy and a mugger killed my parents or a drunk driver took them out, would I immediately be fostered out-city because my *environment* had become unsuitable?"

"That's not the same." His face tightening abruptly,

Philip speaks in an oddly clipped voice.

"It's *exactly* the same!" I put my fork down with a clatter, the surging fear and anger stripping away my appetite.

Face gone ghostly-pale, Susannah puts a—now-shaking—hand on my arm. "They *won't* see it that way, Harry. We're just...we're just worried you don't understand that."

Why are they *this* bothered by what I said? But my eyes burn, my throat tightens—I push her hand away and jerk to my feet. "You city-folk have sent Josh to *prison* for *kidnapping*! But it's you who're the real kidnappers! If that judge doesn't let us go, *he* belongs in jail!"

I run to my room and slam the door as hard as I can, but it doesn't make me feel any better. They *really* think the judge will refuse Mau custody? I know Darryl's worried about the outcome, though she tries to be calm about it, but I haven't wanted to believe it was really in much doubt.

Surely they have to give us back to Mau? Surely, surely, surely, surely, surely?

DARRYL

"...I was hoping to see Darryl. Is she in?"

I'm crossing the landing toward the games room

when the deep voice from the direction of the front door makes me jerk to a halt. I leap to the head of the stairs, peering down.

Father Ben!

"She is, but…I'll have to ask you to wait here for a moment while I clear it with her caseworker."

Ugh, no! I dodge out of sight as Ms. Williamson heads for her office, then run lightly down the stairs. Very, very quietly, I operate the front door latch and ease it open far enough to slip out, closing it even more quietly.

"Darryl!" He's dressed in his usual black pants and shirt, with a clerical collar, and his teeth gleam against his dark skin as he smiles.

"Father Ben!" I throw my arms around his neck. He's been my parish priest since I was just a kid, and the big hug he gives me in return is very welcome. "Father Ben, are you okay? I'm *so* sorry…"

He waves this away. "Darryl, it's fine. I got to do three months of impromptu prison ministry, that's all. I think the warden was sorry to see me go. Prison chaplain certainly was."

I laugh. He seems calm and healthy-looking, thank God, totally unruffled by his misadventure.

"Were you with Josh?"

He shakes his head. "Sorry. I was in some minimum security, standard out-city prison and they never put hunters in those, however minor their offences."

Hunters are kept in the much rarer in-city prisons, since the wilderness that acts as the main form of containment for out-city prisons isn't considered effective with them. The wilds sure would be more of an attraction to Josh than a deterrent. If he could get through the fence, he'd be gone.

"Do you know if he's okay?"

"They only released me yesterday. So far the bishop dragged me all over the mat and told me to get back to work pronto, and that's it. I've booked to visit Josh tomorrow before I head off, but I wanted to see you and Harry first, if I could. I reckon the best gift I can take him is news of you two."

His words lodge a lump in my throat. "Yeah... I'm really worried about him, Father Ben. You know how he hates the city. And the girls say it ain't good to be in prison on any charge relating to what city-folk see as children—guys like that get beaten and murdered and stuff." I glance at him in sudden alarm. "You really *were* okay?"

He smiles reassuringly. "I was fine, Darryl. And I think Josh will be okay on that score—any other hunters in there will have his back, y'know?"

Assuming there *are* any in there... "But he'll be one of the youngest guys in there. The girls say that's bad, too."

"He'll be okay. No one wants to mess with hunters, Darryl."

But in my mind, I hear Josh refusing to allow Harry or me to roam alone in the dark at the midwinter fair: *I guess you're both old enough to know this, but—no way, no how do I know everyone here and not all people are good, right?*

No one but hunters at that fair. And however much hunters grumble about city-folk assuming the worst of them and handing down harsh sentences, most hunters don't end up in jail for nothing at all. So who'll protect him from the protection?

But Father Ben and I may not have long, so I push the worry away and grope in my pocket for that precious rosary that I've been anxiously guarding for the last three months. "Can you give him this? It was his dad's—I bet he'd like to have it. I took it from the 'Vi to keep it safe."

"I'll give it to him." He carefully places it in his own pocket. "How are *you*, Darryl? And Harry?"

"We're okay. I mean, I won't lie, we hate the city, but Uncle Mau should get custody of us real soon, if there's any justice."

Father Ben winces. "You really think so?"

"I *hope* so. The lawyer's got all Dad's paperwork—"

The door opens and Ms. Williamson looks out. "Ah, Darryl. Why am I surprised?" She turns to Father Ben.

"Father Benedict, I have to ask: are you intending to have contact with Mr. Wilson?"

Father Ben shoots me an apologetic look before answering honestly. "Yes, I am."

"Then, I'm sorry; in that case Ms. Matthews absolutely refuses to allow you to have contact with Darryl or Harry."

"*What?*" I explode.

"It's her decision, Darryl, not mine."

"That's *ridiculous*—"

"You can take it up with her, but I think we both know how much good that will do."

I grit my teeth together, practically grinding them, and stare off along the street at the coffee shop on the far corner because it's the only way to keep from glaring at Ms. Williamson. 'Cause I know her well enough now to appreciate that this is all *Fernanda*.

"That woman is a twisted, sadistic she-raptor," I mutter at last.

"Or excessively out of touch with you country-folk," murmurs Father Ben, fair as always. "I'm sorry, Darryl, it looks like we have to choose. I can visit you and Harry when I'm in-city, or Josh, but not both."

I don't even have to stop and think about it. "Josh. He must need a friendly face so bad by now. *No one* will have been in to see him or even made contact, for fear of the city-folk implicating them."

"Well, that train's left the station as far as I'm concerned," jokes Father Ben.

"Exactly. So it needs to be you."

"I agree. Regretfully. Well, if Maurice gets custody…" He trails off and it's clear he doesn't believe it's going to happen. "Well, you'll be eighteen in August," he says more brightly. "So, well—until then."

"Bad idea," says Ms. Williamson quietly.

Father Ben and I swing around to look at her. "Why?" I ask.

"You'll be seeking custody of your little brother, I presume?" I nod, so she goes on, "The last thing you'll want to do is immediately resume keeping company with anyone connected to your time on the run. They considered that an unsafe environment for you both, remember? Any suggestion you'll take your brother back into that environment…" She trails off, raising an eyebrow meaningfully.

Outage, is that true? The first thing I want to do once I've got custody of Harry is to head 'back into that environment.' To the farm, at any rate. Will they distinguish between a farm and a HabVi? Probably not. Is she saying that any suspicion of that will be enough to get my application turned down?

I sure hope Mau gets custody, then, 'cause it may be even harder for me to get it than I thought—and I wasn't assuming it would be *easy*.

But Mau...Mau *lives* in that 'environment.'

Are Harry and I fooling ourselves to even hope?

HARRY

I guess by this point it's not *really* a surprise that the judge rejects Mau's application for custody—and emphatically. Darryl got to go to court with Mau, because she's older. She said Mau was so angry afterward, as angry as she'd ever seen him. He shouted at his lawyer, then apologized to him, then hugged Darryl. Then he shouted some more, at the no-longer-present judge. And then he just hugged her again and begged her to forgive him for failing. On the point of tears, she said. Which is horrible to picture. Darryl was practically crying when she told me. He can't petition again for one year, apparently.

It's a nightmare. Still...

"*You* can get custody as soon as you're eighteen, right?" That's in August, only another few months, now.

"I hope so."

Why does she sound so unsure? "You're my *sister*. Surely *that* should be a done deal?"

"Since when is anything 'surely' where city-folk are involved?"

Too right. I just can't *believe* they turned Mau down.

Except I can. Because that's what they're like. And we're at their mercy.

DARRYL

I lie on my bunk, carefully picturing Josh's face in my mind, as I do at least once a day, since I have no photo of him. I don't think I'd forget what he looks like in nine months—or even a year—but the thought is too horrible.

No school today—it's Saturday. I've already been for the longest run I'm allowed and zipped through all my schoolwork—so repetitive. I've never been one to be bored, but I am with this city-life. I just want to see a real expanse of greenery or blue sky or something alive that isn't human, dog, pigeon, or rat. Huh, if I feel like this, with all my comparative freedom, what's it like for Josh?

My mind turns back to what Ms. Williamson said the other week. It's been bothering me. Really bothering me. Is she right? That they won't give me Harry if they think we'll return to a country environment? I'm behaving myself ever so hard, and so is Harry, but it'll all be for nothing if that's true. What can we do?

I guess once Josh is released, Harry and I could sneak out of the city and we could all make a run for another state, the way we intended before. But if we got caught, they'd send Josh back to prison—and me as well?—and it would mean dumping the farm on Maurice and Riley and Sandra for over three more years until we could return to Exception when Harry turned eighteen, without even the possibility of us taking back responsibility sooner, which isn't right...

"Hey, there's a hunter woman coming up the steps!" exclaims Fei, peering out the window. "At least, I think she's a hunter..."

Kerri and Marnie join her and I go to look too, but the woman's close to the door now, out of our line of sight. I hurry from the room, and I'm soon peeping down the last flight of stairs into the hall.

"Hi, I'm a friend of Darryl's." Is it...*Trudi*? West's girlfriend? I only met her a couple of times at the midwinter fair. I glimpse black-brown skin quite dark enough to be hers but can't get a good look... "Is she around?"

I hurry down the stairs and join Ms. Williamson at the door. Yep, it's Trudi, all right. Dressed in plain khaki rather than camo—newish looking gear, too. She's obviously—to me—trying to look somewhat city-eyes-civilized. She's not even wearing a hunting knife at her belt, despite the old country joke that goes:

What do you call a hunter with an eight-inch knife?
Dressed.

"Darryl!" Trudi opens her eyes and arms wide,

beaming as though we've been friends for years as she enfolds me in a hug. "It's so long since I've seen you!"

I play along, hugging her and beaming too. "Trudi! It's so good to see you! How are you? Ms. Williamson, this is Trudi Harman."

Trudi waggles her ring finger at me, where a simple metal band gleams. "Mrs. Trudi West, now." Unlike Thiago and Ed, West's given name is actually his surname. No mystery why—his first name is Pachycephalosaurus.

"You got married!" I give my hands a little clap together, trying my best to imitate Fei receiving news of her favorite band, and turn to Ms. Williamson with all the bubbly innocent enthusiasm I can muster. "Oh, please say we can have a good chat and she can tell me all about the wedding!"

"There's a little coffee shop just up the street," says Trudi in her calm, easy way. "I were wondering if I could take Darryl there?"

Ms. Williamson eyes me narrowly, and Trudi too. I know Trudi's in her mid-thirties, but with her smooth skin and dark braided hair, she could easily be taken for much closer to my age. And Ms. Williamson has been talking about all the relaxations that should be coming my way if I keep behaving so well.

"Ms. West..." Ms. Williamson says at last.

"Trudi."

"Trudi, have you recently had any contact or intend to have any contact with Mr. Wilson?"

"Joshua Wilson, is that?" Trudi shakes her head casually. "Nope and nope. I don't know him well."

Ms. Williamson eyes us some more. Finally, she nods. "Alright. The two of you may go to the coffee shop for an hour or two. Don't be late for dinner, though, Darryl."

I don't try to hide how pleased I am, smiling at her. "Thanks!"

I head down the steps with Trudi, no doubt sparking a fresh round of commentary up in the bedroom, but I keep quiet until we're well out of earshot of the home.

We pass several people and one familiar dog with a typical nervy city-owner in tow before I say, "Uh...congratulations!"

Trudi smiles. "Thanks." She shoots me a look. "It were a relief to find out why West were dragging his heels so much over proposing, I can tell you."

"He's told you all about it, now, then?" Poor West didn't want to ask Trudi to marry him while there was a chance he could be charged with being an accessory to what Josh was up to.

"Sure did. Moment he could."

We've almost reached the little strip of shops where the cafe nestles. I follow Trudi in, and she leads me straight to the tucked away rear corner, where...yep, West, Thiago, and Ed are seated at a table. They rise to give me quick hugs, bashfully brushing away my thanks for the Easter eggs.

"Trudi did the chocolate, we just painted 'em," says West, shrugging.

"No, you two sit at that table there," says Thiago, indicating the neighboring one as we move to join them. "If someone looks in, you're not sitting with us, then."

It's a sensible precaution, though if Ms. Williamson does wander along to check on me, she'll probably be suspicious of a tableful of hunters that just happen to be sitting not only in the same cafe, but right beside us. Still, suspicion ain't proof.

"So, how are you? How's Josh?" asks West, reaching across to twine hands with his new bride and give her a 'thank-you-you're-amazing' smile that's doubly sweet on the face of such a tall, broad guy.

I sigh. "I don't have the slightest idea how Josh is. My horrible caseworker won't let me know *anything* about him. I wouldn't even know what his sentence was if the lady who runs the home didn't actually have a heart. He's got twelve months but might be out in nine."

They all nod. "We know that from the news," says Thiago. "Just don't know how he *is*. We feel lousy about it, but we haven't dared go near him."

"I doubt he'd want you to," I say quickly, seeing the guilt in their eyes. "If the city-folk did want to cast their net wider, you'd be jumping right into it."

West sighs. "That's the way we figure it, but knowing how Josh is when he's in-city—well, we feel like scum, I can tell you."

"There's no way he'd want you in trouble too. That would only make him feel worse. You're doing the right thing."

"They do know that, in their heads," says Trudi, rolling her eyes. "They just enjoy beating themselves up over it."

"Hey, whose side are you on?" West shakes her hand gently—she just laughs at him.

"And you and Harry?" asks Ed, peering through his blond bangs with unusually anxious blue eyes. "You okay?"

"Yeah. They separated us, as I guess you know."

"Yeah, we got the addresses from your neighbors."

"Right. Well, they won't give Maurice custody—that looks like a lost cause. And now..." I break off, swallowing hard as my throat tightens. "Well...I was hoping to get custody once I'm eighteen, but the housemother thinks I won't get it if there's the slightest indication I'm likely to take Harry out-city. And...after the way they were about Mau...I think she's right. So now I...I don't even know what to do."

My voice shakes; I'm barely holding it together. Trudi releases her husband's hand and takes mine instead, squeezing gently.

"Other than wait for Josh to be free, anyway," I hurry on, "and decamp to another state with him, if he wanted to go. But that burns so many bridges *and* drops all our responsibilities *and* means waiting six months or more *and* we both hate it here *and* Harry's starting to get bullied at school, so...so I just...*don't know what to do.*"

West frowns. Ed wrinkles up his face sympathetically.

Thiago just shrugs. "Clear as clear what you need to do."

"It is?"

"Sure. Just see it as a hunting problem. So, what's the prey? What d'you want?"

"Harry and me to be back on our farm." Do I? Rather than being in-city, yes. But if I had a totally free choice... I push thoughts of Josh and the HabVi from my mind. There's no chance of that anytime soon.

"And how do you get that?"

"Get custody?"

"And how do you get *that*?"

"Um...convince—" Suddenly I see where he's going with this! "—*convince* the city-folk I'm *not* likely to go out-city!"

"Exactly." He smirks at me. "See. It's a stalking

exercise. You just need a different kind of camouflage, that's all."

West grins. Ed slaps Thiago on the shoulder. "Thiago's the brains of the outfit, no mistake."

"Someone's gotta be," smirks Thiago.

So how am I gonna go about this?

"Better be subtle about it," cautions West. "Or they'll guess you're laying a false trail."

"Yeah. Hey, thanks, Thiago; you guys. This really could be the solution."

"Well, we're rooting for you," says Ed. Then becomes distracted by something wriggling inside his jacket. He unzips it a little and a bunny's head pops out, all snuffling nose and silky long ears. "Oh, uh, you wanna baby rabbit, Darryl?"

His casual question is too much. I laugh. I laugh so hard I end up sobbing. Finally I mop my eyes and grin at him. "I would *love* the bunny, Ed. This place is like an animal *void*. But I can't. Ms. Williamson would find out, and it would be sent to the pound."

"I'll keep it, then. I didn't actually bring it for you; I just had it in here."

Normal behavior for Ed, so no surprise there.

"I bet Harry would love a piranha'saur, though. Or even the bunny, come to that. I wonder if his foster-folks would let him keep one? They're the type that Tidies were named after, one hundred percent."

"We were thinking of trying to see him next time we were in-city, if you were allowed to meet Trudi today."

"Please try. He'd be so happy to see you! I think he's having a worse time than me, in a way." Mau did offer to bring Kiko back for Harry, after the disastrous custody hearing, but I vetoed it. Kiko's too social to be left all day while Harry's at school and too shy to take along, even assuming it was allowed, which I reckon it wouldn't be. But piranha'saurs are quite happy to lie on the bed napping all day long until their owner comes back and feeds them again.

"We'll give it a go, then," says West.

"And how are you guys? Did you get your camp set up yet?" Something else we were delaying, since West wanted to propose to Trudi first.

"Sure did," beams West. "Nice little place out in the foothills to the north-west. There were two old buildings on the site already. Trudi and I are doing up the worse one, Thiago took the other."

"Got my mom moved in already." Thiago nods as he speaks, an unusually cheerful look on his face. "And the change actually seems to have done her good—I was afraid it might be too much for her."

"We've almost finished our annex now," West adds, "so my folks will be moving in soon, as well. My dad's gonna retire from his job as an assistant and be an able-bodied campkeeper, so it'll feel like a proper camp, soon, all different generations."

"And Ed?" I ask. Isn't Ed the camp boss, owning fifty percent?

"I'm building a nice little house from scratch," says Ed, still stroking his bunny's soft ears.

"Well, in theory," says Thiago. "So far he's put up quite a few hutches and kennels and things that he can't even use until there're a few more campkeepers and campmakers about to look after whatever's in 'em when we're off hunting."

Yep, sounds like Ed.

Ed shrugs, unconcerned. "The house is coming on just fine. I'll have some nice photos to show Anhar at midsummer."

"That's the woman he was mooning over at the midwinter fair," Thiago tells me, not particularly under his breath.

"Yeah, I remember."

I'd *love* to go to the midsummer fair, but I guess there's no point even thinking about it. I won't be allowed out-city, and even if I was it would wreck my brand new plan to get custody of Harry.

And nothing must be allowed to harm *that*.

HARRY

"I still can't *believe* you're dressed like that."

Honestly, I wasn't expecting *much* from my birthday this year, but I never imagined Darryl would come out of the home head to toe in city-gear when we collected her earlier. Has she suddenly gone native?

Darryl glances over her shoulder. Susannah and Philip are reading an info board at the other end of the velociraptor pen's ObsoDeck. I know they mean well, bringing us to the zoo for a special birthday treat, but it feels like having salt rubbed into a raw wound. Especially the *velociraptors*. Poor Tiny...

"Relax, Harry," Darryl says in a low voice, clearly satisfied Susannah and Philip won't hear. "I haven't had time to fill you in yet. It's all part of The Plan."

"What plan?"

"The plan to get custody. Ms. Williamson—bless her—tipped me off that the custody board will have to believe we plan to stay in-city before they're likely to grant me custody of you."

"What?" My eyes widen in horror. Oh yeah, this birthday just keeps getting better and better. "But that's the last thing we—"

"It ain't impossible, Harry. I saw Technicolor last Saturday—"

"*What?*"

"I'd have told you if I'd seen you properly on

Sunday, but they dragged you off to that educational thing straight after church." She glances over her shoulder again, checking on 'them,' then rushes on, "so, in a piranha'saur egg, West and Trudi got married and they've all set up their camp. I can tell you more about that later; it ain't a secret. But they really helped me thrash out this custody problem. All I have to do is make it look like I'm thoroughly settled in city-life, and the board probably won't even question it. You know what they think about out-city living—can't understand why anyone would want to do it if they had a choice."

"But *how* will you—"

"*Shhh.*"

I fall silent as Susannah and Philip stroll up to us.

"I had no idea raptors were such good parents," says Susannah, smiling and shaking her head. "This is all so interesting."

"*I* had a raptor chick," I snap, unable to hold my tongue. "*I* was gonna be a good parent, too, but a cop threw it into the bushes to die when they kidnapped us."

Susannah's eyes widen in horror—Philip looks uncomfortable.

"I'm sure it isn't very safe for...for *people* to be raising raptor chicks..." he says hesitantly.

"They're about as dangerous at that age as a *duckling*," I snarl, and march off to the other end of the

ObsoDeck.

This birthday totally stinks.

DARRYL

Probably best to give Harry some space. I lean on the fence as Susannah and Philip stare anxiously after my brother. "Let him cool down," I suggest. "He's still awful sore about Tiny. Poor little chick. He was only a few days old. It was a really nasty thing that cop did, making us abandon him like that."

They fidget uncomfortably, their natural abhorrence of harming baby creatures obviously warring with their city-horror of raptors.

"Well, the zoo seems to have lots of chicks." Susannah speaks a little too brightly, gazing down into the pen.

"Sure do. Three nesting pairs." Three abandoned nest mounds dot the enclosure below. With the chicks hatched out, the raptor families have relocated to the open-fronted 'caves' that have been provided for nursery dens. The closest pair, a mature yellow-ruffed female and a much younger, unusually silky-feathered male, watch over their six chicks with what probably looks like close attention to the city-folk, but has a lazy air to my eye. If threats never materialize, even animals tend to relax.

"You see the yellow-ruffed female?" I say.

"Uh...I see a yellow-ruffed *raptor*," says Susannah. "The one in the cave?"

"Yeah. I think she's the matriarch."

They look blank. "How do you know that?" asks Philip.

"Just the way the others act around her. She's pretty old to be matriarch, but her mate's super young and healthy, which could be influencing it subtly."

"It could?" Blank looks.

"Sure. Male hierarchy is separate from female—but mated pairs back each other up big time, so when it comes to the matriarch's mate, it can get a bit confusing."

HARRY

Darryl's leaning on the pen fence, answering Susannah and Philip's questions and watching the raptors with every sign of enjoyment. I'm glad someone's getting pleasure out of this birthday torture...sorry, treat.

Okay, I felt happy enough about the idea when Susannah first mentioned it. But I didn't realize it would be this hard.

The day doesn't improve. The stegosaurs and triceratops remind me of life in the 'Vi with Josh—hard work, but safe in our little family unit. No older boys ramming me with their shoulders and trying to trip me in the school corridors, their eyes promising worse to come. Yates was supposed to come along today, but he cancelled at the last minute. He's been keeping away from me more and more since the mouse incident—scared of those bullies, I think. Or maybe of me.

Darryl rattles on to Susannah and Philip, all sorts of interesting stuff about the critters, sounding like a perfect little huntress. You'd think she was hunter-born.

On to the more commonly domesticated breeds like iguanodons and edmontosaurs—though the zoo's info boards swear these are from wild bloodlines. Darryl gives Susannah and Philip a talk on Farming 101 while I stand and stare at the iggies, hoping no one notices the hot tears pricking the corners of my eyes. I want to be back on the farm so bad. Memories fill my head, of normal life with Dad and Darryl, before this nightmare started. Why? Why was he taken? We still don't know. Will we ever know? Will I be stuck with Susannah and Philip until I'm eighteen?

I mean, I *do* care about them now and they try *so* hard, but they're not my family and even after all these months, they don't understand me at all—and I barely understand them, either. I guess there must be far worse foster-parents, but I just...

...I just wanna go *home*.

DARRYL

Harry makes a sudden dash for the nearby restroom block and my heart sinks. He's not been enjoying this at all, but I don't know what to do other than try to keep Susannah and Philip occupied to give him some privacy.

Strange, in the car, Harry was positive about the idea of the zoo, and it was me who was having butterflies and wondering if it would just remind me of everything we've lost. But, actually, it's really good seeing all the critters. It's been so long, even the zoo stock are better than nothing. A breath of reality. *Our* reality. Or the reality we want. A reminder. Gives me hope.

Harry isn't seeing it that way, clearly. Hunters — so we learned over our year with Josh — are unexpectedly relaxed about tears when they see a cause for them. Their main taboo — and a strong one — is breaking down and crying when there's danger afoot. But farmboys — not quite so relaxed. Tat city-boys even less so. Harry won't want anyone to see him cry.

By the time I've persuaded Philip not to go in after Harry, a zookeeper is giving a talk about snakes and reptiles at a nearby education point and we gather to listen. I keep an eye on the restrooms, though. When I finally see Harry emerge, I slip away to join him, leaving the Jeffords engrossed by the sight of the huge—I hope well-fed—python coiling around the zookeeper's body.

"You okay?"

"Fine."

I don't press the issue. His eyes are still slightly red and I know he ain't fine and he knows I know, but nothing either of us can say will fix it.

His eyes dart around, fixing on his foster-parents, there at a safe distance. "So, how are you gonna lull the custody board? You were about to say…"

"Little steps until I'm eighteen. I'll just dress like a city-girl—that's why I went shopping with my roommates and got these clothes. I'll start to do some of the things city-girls do. And then once I'm eighteen, I'll get an apartment with space for you and a job that will keep us, and the city-folk will assume I'm all settled and, y'know, *cured*. As they see it."

"And they give you custody!"

"That's The Plan."

"Well, that shouldn't be hard, right?"

I hesitate. I want to comfort him, especially since it's his birthday, but I also don't want to give him a false idea about how long The Plan might take. "The first job I can get isn't necessarily going to pay enough to keep us both. Probably won't. If there's a decent amount in Dad's account when I get access, that will help, at least with securing the apartment. And we'll get a little from the farm, though most of the profit has to go to Mau and Riley and Sandra since they're doing all the work."

"Josh has our wages saved."

"Yeah, but that won't be much. We only took the bare minimum of contracts while we were with him. I'm just saying. Even with this plan, I can't say exactly how long it's gonna take."

His face falls a little at that, but his eyes remain brighter. "At least it's an actual plan. It was all so vague before. All that *hopefully you can get custody*. Now we can— Oh, watch out..."

The snake-keeper has concluded his talk without becoming the snake's dinner, and Susannah and Philip are approaching with broad smiles on their faces.

"How about some lunch before we start on the mammals?" says Philip. "Let's head to the food plaza. Harry, you're the birthday boy. You can choose."

DARRYL

I yank on my braid in frustration, scrolling up and down the list of job descriptions on the school's 'My Perfect Job' app that's supposed to match you to your ideal field of employment. My results are all stuff like:

Veterinary staff – but even the junior assistants need a degree!

Landscape gardeners – degree or make a legally

binding commitment to a three-year apprenticeship on a minimum wage.

Zoo staff – degree or have to start at the bottom as an unpaid intern.

And so on, right down to the most coveted city-job of all:

SPARKie—the Fence Maintenance Brigade itself.

I click to close the results and examine the questionnaire again. Can I get it to give results based on salary and ease of entry into the profession instead of according to my preferences?

Yes.

My heart sinks as I scroll down, though I'm not at all surprised. The easy to enter professions—waitress, store staff, warehouse staff—have low wages and slow or limited opportunities to advance quickly.

The well-paid work is only slightly better than my 'perfect' job list. High entry requirements and extremely competitive.

From the look of this, it could take me *months* to be able to afford to keep Harry to the satisfaction of a court, even knuckling down to some grim job that doesn't suit me. I might not even manage it before he's eighteen! *The Plan* is starting to look super rocky.

Then again, we *will* have that farm income, however little. It'll have to help. And surely Dad had some savings? I push my despondence away. I'm far better off than a lot of high school graduates in my position. *Far* better off. I just need to be grateful for that and get the best job I can. It doesn't really matter what the job is, since I'm only planning to stay in it for as long as it takes to secure Harry's freedom.

Mau and Riley are driving up to Exception City on the weekend to take me through the farm accounts. I'll have a better idea of figures after that.

HARRY

"Is it true what they say about country girls?" Allosaur—I still don't know his name—leans close to my ear and follows up with something obscene about Darryl that I'm glad I don't catch properly. What I do hear is enough to clench my fists and teeth tight.

Calm, Harry. Don't react. Hunters don't rise to stuff like that.

Farmers sometimes do...

But I'm not that dumb. Allosaur is over a head taller than me, twice as broad, and trailed by his usual pack of similar-sized cronies. Somehow I manage to keep walking along the school corridor, ignoring him. He wouldn't be this brave if I had my rifle and hunting knife!

He yanks on my bag. I can't help stumbling back into him, hard. He grabs me at once, shoving me into an empty classroom. "Step on my foot like that, would you? You like stomping on things, don't you?"

I dunno why he even bothers trying to act like this fight is my fault. Though it's hardly going to be a fight, is it? His buddies are following us in and shutting the door, their eyes hot and eager.

I back away, watching Allosaur warily, my heart pounding as he looms in front of me, blocking the light from the window. I'd almost be glad to finally get this over with, except it *won't* be over after this. It'll just happen again. And again. And—

Allosaur lunges with a big fist. I manage to dodge. Another lunge. Another dodge. I'm faster than him. One of his friends laughs. Allosaur's cheeks flush with anger. I try to avoid getting near the cronies, but eventually I have to dodge that way. One of them pushes me hard, sending me staggering. Allosaur's fist lands in my stomach a second later, driving the breath from me. Struggling to draw in air against the pain, I try to dodge again, but his next punch hits me in the side, followed by a kick to my leg that folds it and drops me to the floor.

"Not so tough now, huh?" His sneering face hovers over me as he kicks me again and again. I curl into a ball, protecting my head with my hands, though it seems he isn't quite stupid enough to kick me *there*. "Not so t—"

He breaks off at a whistle from one of his friends and suddenly they're piling back out into the hall, faces carefully pointed away from whoever's approaching, like they're thick enough to think that'll stop them being recognized. I mean, one of them has a tattoo on the back of his neck, for pity's sake!

I lie still, panting in pain, barely holding back tears of shame. Irrational tears. He's so much bigger than me and has his friends to help. It wasn't a fair fight. Not a fight at all. Just raptors ganging up on their prey.

The comparison doesn't make me feel any better.

DARRYL

I'm crossing the hall with Kerri, wishing that the most modest city-dress I could find was just a little longer on the leg, when Ms. Williamson appears in the office doorway.

"We've got permission!" blurts Kerri at once. "Remember?"

"Movie theatre, no boys, got it. Darryl, I'm sorry, Ms. Jefford called. Harry got beaten up at school today, and she wondered if you'd like her to come and collect you so you can try to cheer him up."

Kerri's face falls. She already bought the tickets for us after school and she won't be allowed to go solo— and I haven't given her the money yet.

"I must go and see Harry," I say apologetically. "Ms. Williamson, could you tell her yes?"

Ms. Williamson nods and heads back into the office.

"If you can find someone who'll pay for the ticket, then great," I tell Kerri, who's glowering. "Otherwise, I'll pay you for it, but give it to anyone who'll go with you, okay?"

Kerri brightens. "Thanks, Darryl." She high fives me. I don't blame her for being surprised. There are a lot of girls here who'd refuse to pay up if they couldn't go, and honestly? Kerri's probably one of them.

HARRY

"What the heck?" *whispers Darryl as we finally clear the ridge.*

I'm staring just as hard. An honest-to-God city-car lies crumpled against a cliff-side only some five hundred feet away. It sports the usual lightweight grilles city-folk fit for inter-city travel and has snow chains on the puny little tires…but all the same. How did they even get that up here?

They're not going any further, that's for sure. Steam streams sideways from under their scrunched-up hood and, even as I watch, a large male pachysaur hurtles over the snow and smashes its huge domed head full force into the passenger door, punching clear through it. Panicked yells from inside as the pachy backs away again, now wearing the door on its shoulders like an oversized necklace. Yeah, now they're stationary, the pachys can do a lot more damage, a lot faster. Whoever's in that car hasn't long.

"Bachelor gang," says Josh on the intercom. "That looks like the leader. Drop it, one of you, quick."

Yeah, two more male pachys, one almost as large as the first and one a little smaller, are already scuffing their feet in the way that means they're about to charge…

I adjust my aim, but Darryl's rifle cracks before I can get off a shot. The door-stealing pachy topples onto rock and snow with a clang and a thud and lies twitching until a bullet each from Darryl and me finishes it off. The others—about five of them—startle at the shots, tiny eyes peering through the snow. But I guess they've never been hunted, because the larger of the two decides the—badly wind-muffled—noises are nothing to worry about and charges anyway. I track it for a second until sure, then fire at the exact same time as Darryl. I guess we both hit it—it drops to the ground, anyway, and doesn't move at all.

The 'Vi's horn and lights activate as Josh finally manages to spare a hand from the wheel. Darryl and I both jump, and faced with this onslaught of the unfamiliar, the pachys turn tail and bolt. They are herbi'saurs, after all, however unpleasantly territorial. No meal at stake for them, here.

Josh's voice comes over the Intercar instead of the intercom, very firm. "Occupants of the blue city-car, remain where you are until we tell you to move."

Only moments later the hatch lifts and he's climbing up, rifle in hand. "Okay, let's get those city-idiots over here before any hungry raptors show up," he says, shaking his head in disgust.

Yeah, that car is beyond *compromised!*

I wake with a jolt that makes me whimper slightly. I'm alone, so it doesn't matter...oh.

"Hi, Harry." Darryl peers anxiously at me. "Are you okay?"

"I was back in the 'Vi. It was real nice. Then I woke up."

She gives me a sympathetic smile. "Heard you got bashed around today?"

I sigh. A teacher found me before I could scrape myself off the floor and called Susannah to come collect me early. I'd hardly have been able to hide what had happened, anyway, limping and with a split lip.

"Does the school have any plan to make sure this doesn't happen again?" Darryl asks grimly, looking like she's gonna march in there and have words with them if the answer's no.

"No need for you to do anything." I grin, then regret it when my lip starts bleeding again. "Susannah already blew up on them. Said I'd finished my certificate for the year so I wouldn't be going back until next semester, which should, I quote 'give them plenty of time to sort out their school's *serious problems.*'"

Darryl breathes out a sigh of relief. "Well, that's a temporary fix."

"I'm gonna start looking for a part-time job immediately. Help out with"—I lower my voice—"*The Plan*. But I'm gonna start next year's certificate on my TuteApp as well, see if I can get Susannah and Philip used to me homeschooling. Then maybe they'll change their mind about sending me back at all. Apparently, because they're my foster-parents they actually get more say than Fernanda."

Darryl nods. "That's a real good idea. Because I don't see how I can have you out of here before the next semester, however hard I try. I doubt I'll even be ready to petition the court by then. I don't even move out of the home until after my birthday in August."

August... "Wow, I can't believe that's in only a month and a half! Are you excited?"

Darryl shrugs, looking grim again. "Honestly? I still don't really feel like I know the city very well and finding a job and then an apartment is intimidating. But Kerri and Ms. Williamson say they'll help, so it will be fine."

"Oh, what did Mau and Riley and Sandra say? They popped in to see me on Saturday, afterward, but no business talk." My stomach drops suddenly. "Oh no, was that okay? If I see country-folk without the excuse you've got—managing the farm—it won't harm *The*

Plan, will it?"

Darryl shakes her head. "If *I* saw them without reason it would. But you can do what you like."

"You sure?"

"Oh yeah. It's me the court's going to be looking at, because I'll be the adult who's making the decisions. Anyway, like you said, *you've* got foster-parents, who're responsible for you. Unless Fernanda gets someone explicitly banned from having contact with you"—a shadow crosses her face—thinking of Josh and Father Ben?—"it's up to Susannah and Philip who you're allowed to socialize with. Even Fernanda isn't going to make a list of every single person we ever knew before we came in-city and have the court 'no-contact' them all."

I breathe out in relief. "Good. Oh, uh, what did Mau and Riley and Sandra say?"

Darryl nods, pursing her lips. "It's not too bad. I mean, we're not talking big money, but they—quite honestly, they're both taking only a very modest remuneration. I just *had* to offer them a bigger percentage, but they both refused. So there's more for us than there might be. It'll definitely help."

From the shadow on her face, I've a nasty feeling it won't be *enough*, though. She's gonna have to climb a few rungs in whatever job before it's *enough*, isn't she? My heart sinks like a box of ammo chucked into a river.

There really is no way I'll be out of here before next semester. I knew I wouldn't be. But Allosaur and his gang will still be there so I guess...I guess I was hoping, all the same.

DARRYL

"Oh, you won't believe what Mau gave me," I tell Harry. "Early birthday present, said he wanted me to have it now."

Harry smirks slightly and raises an eyebrow. "Oh yeah? What?"

"Huh, you suggested it, didn't you?"

He grins. "W-e-e-e-ell, he might've sent me a message begging for ideas."

"In that case, thank you as well, Harry. I love it."

Harry's grin fades. "Just don't ask me to go with you."

I give him a reassuring smile. "I won't. We couldn't afford it, anyway. I wouldn't be spending any money at all if it wasn't for trying to look convincingly citified. My behavior while I'm still at the home will be on record, so it's a window of opportunity. Once I move out, the court will have much less idea what I get up to."

"Yeah, it's important," Harry says. "I get that. I don't care, anyway. I don't mind a movie now and then, but I just wish I could..." He trails off, frowning in a way that suggests he doesn't actually know what he wants to do with himself, stuck in here. Not the zoo—the annual pass Mau splurged on for me wouldn't make him happy at all. Not the mall that I now regularly traipse tediously around with Kerri, Fei, and Marnie. Harry doesn't want to do city-stuff any more than I do, but reminders of the country just upset him. Poor Harry.

I almost open my mouth and tell him that West, Thiago, and Ed might come see him, but I stop myself just in time. If they get cold feet and don't show, Harry will be even more down.

HARRY

I put the empty can into my can bag and trundle the shopping cart on its way. Collecting abandoned cans and bottles is tedious, but at least it's outdoors. And *legal*. When I realized how limited the job opportunities were for someone my age, I tried staking out parking lots with a bucket of water, sponge, and squeegee, offering to clean car windshields. Most of the city-cars don't even have grilles in the way. But I got taken back to Susannah and Philip's house in a cop car. Got a lecture, too. Something about needing a license and being too young for one. It's like these people don't think a fifteen-year-old is old enough to work. Crazy.

You get money for every can or bottle you take back for re-use, though. Not much, but it's the only thing I've come up with so far that no one freaks out about.

Disappointment sits like lead in my belly as I hand my afternoon's haul over at the local collection center and get another pitiful sum added to my petty cash card. Is this really all I'm gonna be able to contribute? I know Darryl's going to tell me it isn't worth me walking the streets for hours just for this and I should get on with my TuteApp.

And maybe I should—but even this is better than doing *nothing at all.*

DARRYL

Happily, the zoo is on the same side of the city as the home. Far out on the outskirts, of course, but it's a direct bus ride to get there. Riley and Sandra, bless them, gave me an annual bus pass for that route, so between them my neighbors thought of everything.

The semester finishes at the end of the week, so I'll be able to spend more time here, but so far I've managed to make a short visit several times a week, straight after school on any day I'm not dutifully making like a city-girl. The zoo is usually moderately busy when I arrive, parents taking their kids for a quick peep at the animals. But right before closing time, it gets super quiet as the families head off to get home in time for supper.

I lean on the fence over the edmontosaur pen, waiting for the last mother and child to leave the ObsoDeck. This is my favorite time. Because once I have the place to myself...*yep, they've gone.*

I slide easily over the fence and pick my way down the steep, artificially boulder-strewn bank until I reach the best spot. Somewhat shielded from the ObsoDeck, but not low enough to be unsafe around the stock. Most of the edmos are browsing on a fresh bale of hay in their fake boulder-type feeder, but Moon Princess (how do they come up with the names at this place?) heads my way, hoping for treats—or at least some attention.

"You're a clever girl, aren't you," I tell her, rubbing all down the middle of her face. "You've got me figured out. Hmm, you've got ticks again, haven't you, girl? I should bring a tick puller."

After making her wait a few minutes—very bad training to spoil any animal, especially one this size—I open my satchel and slip her a giant-size economy rabbit chew, all oats and lettuce and the odd bit of dried carrot. Nutritious food for an edmo.

"I know, tiny, but tasty, right? I'm sorry I can't give you any proper-sized treats, but I can't go to the farm store and they'd be real hard to carry. Here, have another."

"Hey!"

I tense as a voice calls from the ObsoDeck. Darn. I turn to look. Yep, some kind of uniform. Well, it was gonna happen eventually. There's no way to hide properly.

"What are you doing down there? Come up immediately."

A keeper, I think. Not a security guard. Is that better or worse?

"Have you got a tick puller on you?" I call.

"What?"

"A tick puller."

"Yeah..."

"Can you toss it down to me?"

After a moment's confusion, he pulls something from his belt and tosses it accurately. I catch it and fish out another treat. "Here, girl. Have another while I do something about these pests."

Fourteen ticks later, I climb up the slope to where the keeper still waits, leaning on the fence as he watches me. I slide over the fence and straighten, handing him his tick puller.

"Thanks. These all came off her head." I hold out a handful of dead ticks. "Plus a few I dropped. Obviously I couldn't get under her chin; she could've crushed my hand against the slope. You need to get them in the race and check them all over, I reckon."

I toss the ticks aside and wipe my hand on my pants before remembering I'm wearing these fancy city clothes. Who cares; they still wash.

"I'll tell their keeper," says the keeper in front of me. "I think they're trialing some new natural tick repellent with all the herbi'saurs. Looks like it may not be a big success."

"Yeah, even the best natural product has to be paired with regular check-overs and occasional applications of something stronger."

The man—fair skin, stocky, middle-aged—is still eyeing me. "You're not the usual silly princess who risks life and limb in the pens. You knew what you were doing. What are you, farmer?"

I shrug. "And a hunter. Kinda both. Living in-city now, though. I like to come and see the stock...uh, the exhibits."

He nods. "Well, you know I've got to say it. Don't do that again. The pens are out of bounds. If you want to get up close and personal you've got to pay for an experience day—or you could apply for one of the school leaver internships. You look about the right age."

I roll my eyes. "Me and the other one thousand applicants per position and then work for almost nothing?"

He gives a wry smile. "That's how it goes, I'm

afraid."

"Yeah, I'd love to, but I have a little brother to keep."

My stomach twists as I realize how much I actually would love to. If I've got to live and work in-city for a while, the zoo is definitely the best place. What if I take some boring job and never manage to earn enough to get Harry back before he's eighteen and I might just as well have applied for the internship?

I shake the thoughts away. No. I refuse to think like that. I'm making it my firm goal to have Harry and me back on the farm by...I want to say Christmas, but within the year is probably more realistic, sadly. My stomach clenches. How many times can Harry get beaten up in a year?

"Shame, you look far more promising than most," says the keeper. His gaze goes back to the pen, and I know he's about to seek some commitment from me *not to do it again.*

I smile brightly, mind racing as I seek a noncommittal response. *Saint Des, help!* I don't want to lose the tiny hint of normality I've just found...

His walkie-talkie makes a noise and he raises it to his ear. "Yes? Ned here... He's done *what?*"

I mouth a polite "Good evening" and make a hasty escape.

Oh yeah, *Thanks, Saint Des!*

HARRY

"Harry, come have some lemonade when you're done." Susannah stands on the porch holding up a jug.

I raise a hand to acknowledge her, then go back to trundling the mower up and down the final couple of strips of lawn. Yeah, they let me use their 'dangerous' little hand mower now. I think they're slowly getting to grips with what country-kids can do, though I'm still not sure if they really believe I've been towing the full-size grass cutter behind a tractor since I was twelve.

Done. I switch off the mower and head for the porch, wiping my forehead on my arm. It's a hot day. Nearly August, so what do I expect?

I settle on the swinging seat beside Susannah and accept the glass she offers me, sipping eagerly. She smiles at me.

I don't remember Mom very well and having Susannah looking at me like that does feel good, but I can't help asking curiously, "What?"

"Oh, just nice to see you looking happy and relaxed."

"Well, not having to go to school sure helps!"

But her words have soured my mood. Until I remember what Darryl told me, soon after we were brought here: *It's okay if you enjoy some city-stuff, Harry. Doesn't change the fact you want to live in the country. So don't go feeling guilty about it, okay? That would just be dumb.*

Darryl's right. Insisting on being miserable without cause won't get Darryl and me home any faster.

"I've been wondering," I say after quickly draining my glass—mowing is thirsty work today! "Why are you fostering me when you could get some little kid you could adopt and everything?" Susannah's face tenses. Oops. "Sorry, you don't have to—"

"No, of course you wonder about that. We—Philip and I—we had a little girl of our own, actually. But, uh, she was hit by a car when she was four. We...we did try fostering younger kids, but it was too hard. And we realized it was crazy to keep doing that to ourselves when there were so many kids your age who need a family too. So that's why we do older fostering now."

Outage. I just had to ask. Huh, no wonder what I yelled at them that time struck a nerve.

"I'm, uh, I'm real sorry about your little girl." My brain revs frantically—that can't be enough of a response for something like that! Guess nothing is, but... "Uh...what was her name?"

I wanna get off this topic as fast as possible, actually, but it feels like the right question.

Susannah's face melts into a sad but genuine smile. Yeah, I was right to ask. "Susan. She'd be...actually, she'd be almost your age, now. Fifteen in November. I can show you a few pictures when we go inside. We don't put them on the photo frame in the lounge because—well, it's too confusing and complicated, kids arriving here and having to see and hear about that straight-off. Just the one in our bedroom. She's always on there."

"Uh, that's nice... And, um, considerate. Of you."

Susannah looks at me for a moment and smiles. "More lemonade, Harry?"

Change of subject! "Thanks!"

I place my glass on the table and she refills it.

"You know we care about you a lot, Harry, don't you?"

I nod, my cheeks reddening. "Yeah, I...I know that. And...I mean, I care too. About...about you two. I do. Please don't think that I... It's not *you*. I just don't—" *want to be here*, I bite off, 'cause how can that not hurt her feelings?

But she just slips her arm around me and holds me close for a moment. "I know, Harry," she murmurs. "I know."

And I guess she does. But I still don't want to say it to her straight.

DARRYL

"So, Darryl, how are you doing? I hear there are signs that you are adjusting."

It's my birthday in less than a month, now, but I still have to endure one last appointment with Fernanda, oh joy, in her office. She's wearing a turquoise tracksuit, today, as though she's on route to the gym, or maybe just trying to dress casually for some reason. Even her sneakers are turquoise, with cream edging. Her perfume is just as strong as ever. Apple, *again*. She may have put me off apple pie for life.

"I didn't like the city much to begin with," I say frankly, "but I'm enjoying it a lot, now." *When I'm at the zoo*, I add in my head, so it's not quite a lie.

"And what are your plans when you turn eighteen in August, sweetie-pie?"

"I'm looking for a job already, and I'll be getting an apartment soon."

"So you're staying in-city?" Her eyes x-ray me with surprising intensity. Honestly, I thought that when it came to my 'conversion' to city-life Fernanda would lap it up more than anyone. I guess despite her sugary manner she must have a lot of experience with the worst of human nature, in this job.

My stomach tightens, but I speak casually. "It definitely seems best. I never realized how hard and dangerous country-life was until I moved here. And I want to stay near Harry."

"And what *are* your plans with regard to Harry?"

"I'm going to work hard so he can come and live

with me as soon as possible."

Fernanda is still inspecting my face with close attention. I fight to keep it as calm and still as Josh taught me to stay if a T. rex is nearby.

"You understand that for him to live with you, you would need to have custody, dear?"

"Sure, but I am his sister, right? I know there's nothing doing until I have a stable living situation and adequate income, but I absolutely mean to have that as soon as possible."

Fernanda folds her elegant hands together, still eyeing me so closely. "Yes, you *are* his sister. You understand, that means that once you have custody, the state cannot easily take it back from you without significant cause. So, they will wish to be absolutely certain you have your brother's best interests at heart before they grant it to you."

"Naturally." I speak calmly, but my heart is pounding, *thud-thud-thud*. What is she saying?

"With a record like yours" —Fernanda's lips thin— "well, let's just say that were I you, I would prioritize a long-term career over simply *getting enough income quickly*. The court will need to believe you are sincere in your intention to remain in-city."

"I thought I just need to be able to provide for Harry!" I protest, my heart plummeting.

"Ordinarily. But you can be sure that my final

report on your case will make it clear to the court that they need far more substantial evidence of your *genuine* intentions."

"My *genuine intentions*?" I try my best to look bewildered. "I just want my brother back!"

"Very touching, sweetie-pie, but your clothes tell me a different story."

Now I *am* bewildered. "My *clothes*? I...I'm wearing totally normal clothes." *City* clothes.

"Not really, dear. Most girls don't dress exclusively in shades of grey, black, and concrete-beige, as though they're afraid at any moment they might need to blend into the nearest structure and hide."

What the— I can't *believe* she noticed that! I *did* keep trying to put some brighter stuff in my shopping cart, but it felt like a totally different level of betraying what I really am—or want to be. I never thought anyone would *realize* I was wearing subtle city-cam. And these city-streets still make me feel on edge. It seemed safer not to stand out.

"I feel comfortable in these colors. I like them."

She just looks at me.

"A *career* will take ages to establish!" I say. "Are you *trying* to keep me and Harry apart? Don't you realize we're the only family we each have left?"

"Harry is very well off with the Jeffords." Fernanda sounds grimmer than I've ever heard her, burnt sugar instead of oozing syrup. "Unless we can be *absolutely certain* that he will be safe with you, it is far better that he remain right where he is. If you are sincere, Darryl, then focus on a career."

"Harry will be eighteen before I get well-enough established in a *career* job!"

"The fact that you've looked into it thoroughly enough to even *know that* makes me all the more certain Harry should stay put." Fernanda stares at me. "It's very hard to trust a girl who could put on a such a sweet show of compliance and then leave someone, alone, inside a farmhouse in the middle of nowhere, while dragging her little brother into appalling danger not only from the wildlife but also from some random stranger—and a psychologically disturbed *hunter* boy, at that. One might just be left feeling that such a girl could be very two-faced and conniving indeed, to say nothing of her devastatingly poor judgment."

I stare back at her. What's gotten into her? She's always so full of endearments and syrupy words. Is it because today is our last session? She's saying how she really feels for once? But before I've even finished thinking it, the sickly smile is back.

"Darryl, dear, don't misunderstand me. I'm delighted you're making such progress, and I very much hope it is genuine. But I have to think about Harry too, you understand? And with your history..."

She pauses delicately. "Well, I have to err on the side of caution and the court will too. You've only yourself to blame, dear."

Insides churning, seething with anger, I try to keep a calm face. "Of course, Ms. Matthews. Is that all?"

She looks at me for a while longer, and not for the first time I wonder if she can tell how much I dislike her. "Yes, Darryl. That will be all. I wish you luck in your chosen field—whatever it may be."

I make it out of the building, across the busy road, and into the nearby park, managing to nestle myself into the middle of some bushes before I sink down to the ground, put my face in my arms, and sob.

So much for *The Plan*.

How many times will that woman snatch everything from us?

HARRY

I lie on the sofa, staring at the TV without seeing the movie Susannah switched on to "cheer me up." Darryl came over yesterday, Friday, and I've been so down since I got the truth out of her about why *she* was so down. Why she hadn't been over yet, although school's out.

"What are you gonna do?" I asked her.

"I'm gonna stick to The Plan—more or less."

"But—"

"I've been thinking about nothing else for three solid days, Harry, and I don't see what else to do. The way I figure it, I'm never gonna do well enough, fast enough in one of those desirable career jobs even to be ready to seek custody of you within three years. So what's the point? The only hope is to get a good income and seem really stable and settled—maybe wait a little longer than we planned—and then seek custody anyway. And hope the court aren't as paranoid as Fernanda."

I turn on my back, staring at the ceiling. I can't fault Darryl's reasoning. I don't see what else to do either. But that conversation she recounted with Fernanda...is there any hope?

Am I really going to be here for the next three years? I just feel so...so *alone.* Allosaur and his gang aren't going to forgive me for breaking up their Mouse Torture Party any time soon. I mean, if it had been an honest mistake with a pet, I'd have offered to buy them a new one, sure. But the poor critter was better off dead. Most of the boys at school didn't seem to get that—they'd taken to avoiding me and calling me Mouse Slayer or Psycho Stomper, like I just did it to be mean. The ones who'd lurked around me with hopeful, admiring looks sure weren't the ones I wanted to hang with.

Susannah and Philip are kind, but heck, I hate my

life.

"Saint Des?" I haven't prayed as much as I should have, recently. Everything just seems so dark and hopeless, like I'm seeing it through the city-smog. But now I murmur under my breath, "Please help?"

Nothing happens, of course. I stare at the ceiling for a few more...minutes? hours? days?...until finally the doorbell rings. I don't get up. Susannah's already coming out of her home office and what do I care if there's someone at the door?

"Uh, hello?" Susannah sounds uncertain.

A vaguely familiar female voice answers cheerfully, "Hello, are you Mrs. Jefford?"

"Uh...Ms. Jefford, yes, that's me." City folk don't really use Mrs., I've noticed.

"My name's Trudi West and this is my husband Pachy West."

"Just call me West," says a deep voice.

I leap off the sofa and dive around the corner into the hall in my socked feet, almost skidding into the opposite wall. "West!"

"Oh, hey there, cub."

I throw myself into his bear hug, clinging tight and...

Oh heck, I burst into tears. I bury my face against his broad chest to hide it as best I can but, thank God, he's a hunter, so as long as he thinks I've cause he won't think less of me, and nor will Trudi.

"Oh dear," he rumbles, rubbing my back. "You're having a rough year, Darryl tells me."

"Sure am," I sniff. But by the time I manage to get a grip and let go of him, shame heats my stomach.

"I guess I shouldn't complain," I mutter. "I've got food and drink and a roof over my head and Susannah and Philip are real nice and everything." As I turn my head, I glimpse Susannah watching me, her face tight, pain and dismay in her eyes. "I guess I just feel like a plant that's been yanked up by the roots and replanted in a totally unsuitable habitat. And now Darryl's talking about us *living* in-city long-term and that just makes it even worse."

I wink with the eye Susannah can't see so they know I'm talking about The Plan as far as the last bit goes. Except it's a limping, wish-and-a-prayer plan, now, and what I said is too likely the truth. But it's still the best plan we've got, short of hiding in a HabVi and running away again, and no one's gonna go along with that after what happened to Josh, not even Technicolor.

West and Trudi give me sympathetic nods just as Philip peers over Susannah's shoulder.

"Uh, this is Trudi and Pachy West," Susannah says. "Friends of Harry's."

Philip also eyes them doubtfully, though they're wearing single color khaki instead of camo and they've even ditched their belt knives, which is a big sacrifice for a hunter to make. Still perfectly obvious what they are, of course, but I guess they aren't trying to hide *that*, just trying not look too overpoweringly hunter-ish.

"Howdy," says West, holding out his hand politely.

Philip shakes their hands and greets them equally politely, to my relief.

"So, uh, you're here to see Harry?"

"Yeah, we're in-city this weekend and we thought we'd stop by. We were hoping the three of you might like to join us for a cook-out in the 'Vi-park tomorrow lunch-time."

"Really?" I sound as excited as a little kid but I can't help it.

"Sure thing."

"The 'Vi-park?" From Susannah's tone, she might as well be saying 'the alien planet?' Philip looks quietly horrified.

"Just us from my 'Vi and a couple of Trudi's relatives. They've got a few cubs—er, kids—with them about Harry's age. A nice, quiet Sunday gathering."

I turn to Susannah and Philip. "Can we go? Please?"

Philip's jaw firms, then he opens his mouth. He's gonna say no, isn't he?

"Philip?" Susannah places a hand on his arm. Her voice wobbles slightly, but she speaks bravely. "We, uh, we could go along, uh, at least this once, right? I think

Harry would really enjoy it."

I try not to dance from foot to foot as I wait for Philip's reply. His Adam's apple bobs for a moment, before he finally says, "Well...if you would also like to go, honey, I guess..." Another bob. "I guess we can accept the invitation."

"Thank you!" I hug him around the middle, then Susannah, then West. "This is gonna be awesome!"

The 'Vi-park's still in-city, but only just—and I get to hang out with country-folk for an afternoon!

Thanks, Saint Des!

I guess I shoulda spoken to you sooner, shouldn't I?

DARRYL

I lean on the fence, watching the pachys wandering around their pen. The city-folk on the ObsoDeck with me "ooh" and gasp as two males take a run-up and head butt one another, but it's just a minor dominance tiff, not the full impact sparring of the mating season.

Glad of the distraction, I don't try to stop my thoughts from drifting back to that incident with the pachys and the city-idiots...

After only a very brief survey of the surrounding area and no attempt to launch the drone into the teeth of the gale, Josh touches the Intercar again. "Blue city-car, get out and come to the Habitat Vehicle, now. You have cover."

For a moment there's no sound or movement from the badly damaged car and an image fills my mind: Carol, clinging to the steering wheel of our truck in silent terror.

"Move," barks Josh, less sympathetically.

Thank God, a woolly hat appears from the doorless opening, followed by the head it's perched on, which turns into a figure wearing a heavy winter coat and clutching a rifle. The…guy?…plunges into a snowdrift up to his waist and begins to flounder toward the 'Vi. Another figure, similarly dressed and armed, plows after him. And another. Three guys.

"What the heck are they doing out here?" I murmur.

"They're armed, at least," says Harry approvingly.

Josh snorts. "That just increases my certainty that we're about to hear something totally and utterly beyond idiotic. Anyway, keep your eyes peeled. If they got through all that without a scratch on them it's a near miracle. The weather's so wild it will take raptors longer to trace the blood scent — but not that much longer."

Despite the snow and wind, the guys reach the 'Vi pretty quickly. Josh operates the sliding door from the turret, closing it as soon as they're inside, and then we're free to go below and see what we've saved.

With them shivering so violently, stamping and jiggling and slapping their hands together, it's quite hard to make out much about the individual guys. Josh pulls mugs from the cupboard, fills them with boiling water and shoves them their *way. No need to add any cold water since it cools to drinking temperature almost instantly in this weather.*

Dragging their gloves off, the city-guys seize the cups like thirsty men in a desert, though it's the warmth they want more than the liquid, I bet. They're all older than Josh, but not that much older. Early twenties?

Josh is merciful enough to let them finish the mugfuls and settle in the chairs Harry sets up for them before finally demanding, "What in Saint Des's name are you three doing out here?"

The guy who got out of the car first looks Hispanic, curls of dark hair escaping from under his hat. He hugs the empty mug to his shuddering chest, blinking what are probably tears of relief from his eyes, his teeth still chattering.

"We…ugh…we…c-came out to do a spot of…of r-raptor h-hunting."

"After how many beers?" Josh's sarcasm could cut rock.

Heat flushes the guy's light brown cheeks. "A f-few."

"And you got this far before you sobered up?"

A sullen shrug. "W-we'd come far enough we f-figured…we figured we might as w-well keep on now we w-were out here."

Josh lets out an enormous sigh that's as good as a scream of frustration from someone as self-controlled as he is, but contents himself with shaking his head. "Well, you're darn lucky we were here. What those pachys left, the raptors would've finished up."

"What was g-going on with those th-things?" demands the guy who came out second. Curly Afro hair and deep caramel skin peep from under his fleece hat. "We sh-shot at them, over and over, I s-swear we hit them—at least s-some of the time. They d-didn't even s-seem to notice!"

"Oh, they d-did!" protests the third guy, as Hispanic as the first, red-eyed and shaking even harder than the other two. "But they j-just got even m-madder!"

Harry rolls his eyes. "They're pachys! Thickest skulls of any living creature. Shooting them in the head will only cheese them off. How could you not know that if you have even the tiniest aspiration to be hunters?"

"N-not proper hunters," mutters the first guy. "J-just wanted to b-bag some r-raptors. Herbi'saurs are b-boring."

Josh laughs outright, at that. "Well, those boring herbi'saurs almost added you to their bag."

The three guys shudder. "Sure did," mutters the first one.

Josh sighs again. "Ah well, no harm done, 'cept to your car, leastways. Let's get some food on for you guys."

Their heads lift like raptors scenting prey.

"Aw, yeah!" sighs the first.

"A meal would be good," agrees the second.

"I could eat a…a pachy-thingie!" adds the third.

"It'll be iggy steaks," I say briskly.

"And you'll be eating them for several days," says Josh. "Because that's how long it's gonna take to get you back to *civilization by the time this storm lets up."*

Harry shoots him an anxious look and I eye him too. We can't take these guys in-city, right? He just mouths Technicolor. Right. We'll offload them to West and the others.

"Say!" the first guy brightens. "If we'll be with you a few days, how about you take us to do some proper hunting?"

"We can pay," says the Afro guy, whose smart city parka certainly seems to back up that claim.

The third guy blinks uneasily, swallows, and belatedly pastes a rather unfelt look of eagerness on his face when his friends shoot him a look.

"That," says Josh, scooping up a city-guy's rifle from where it's been dumped, "is completely a discussion for another day. Right now"—he picks up the second rifle—"until I see what your weapons handling skills are like"—he seizes the third rifle, just ahead of a belated grab from guy number one—"these *stay* in our gun cabinet. Got it?"

Ignoring the indignant spluttering from the rifles' owners, Josh makes short work of securing them. "Standard 'Vi rules," he says blandly.

"That kid's *holding a rifle!" protests Afro-guy, pointing at Harry, who bristles. "And you look like you barely need to shave, yourself!"*

"I don't care how old anyone is," retorts Josh, "I only care how good their weapons handling skills are…"

An ear-splitting squeal from a nearby child snaps

me back to the present with the usual twinge of loss. *Josh, I miss you. Are you okay?* He might be out in just over three months, but can I see him without risking custody of Harry? Ignore Josh or lose Harry, what kinda choice is that?

Harry was so upset when I filled him in about what Fernanda said. He didn't say much, but he was. I feel like I've let him down, even though it's not my fault. Or is it? Did I not play the city-girl perfectly enough? Should I have dressed up in all kinds of colors? But I figured it would be more convincing if I was as comfortable as possible in my new clothes. If the city-folk would just let me be a good big sister to him and take him home to the farm… As if.

Ugh. Fernanda. She as good as told me she's going to do everything she can to keep me from getting Harry back. What kind of job will ever be good enough, after she's done with her report? The kind it's not even worth thinking about managing to get, is what.

Maybe when Josh gets out, we *should* just run away to another state.

I try to push the thought from my mind, but it's hard. I can't risk getting Josh in trouble again. I can't just dump the farm on Mau and Riley and Sandra.

Yeah? But if I'm gonna be stuck in-city for three years uselessly trying to get custody of Harry, what difference would it even make to them?

A cold feeling wriggles through my belly. Because, logically, if my attempt to get custody fails, surely *I* should go back and run the farm so Mau and Riley and Sandra can concentrate on their own affairs?

And leave Harry behind in the city, completely alone? *No!* And yet, is it fair on our neighbors to leave them responsible for our farm once I'm legally an adult and perfectly able to take care of it myself?

I shudder. I know they'll understand me staying in-city for a while, in order to make an attempt to get Harry back. So I'll cross that other bridge only if we come to it.

HARRY

"Are you sure about this?" I overhear Philip speaking to Susannah as I approach the kitchen on Sunday morning and pause, listening, my insides clenching. "It could be...it could be very *rough* there."

"Mr. West said it would be quiet." Susannah speaks in such a brave voice it makes me want to hug her. "And his wife seemed nice. And it'll be broad daylight. We can always...always *leave*."

"I'm just not sure this is a good idea. Harry's supposed to be getting used to city life. Is this really going to help?"

"Darling, he's such a good boy and he tries so hard

not to upset us, but he's miserable, can't you see that? Ms. Matthews has always made it clear that he'll probably be with us until he's eighteen, but if you ask me, he'll go back to his farm then and nothing that happens in the meantime will change that. The least we can do is allow him to socialize with some country people now and then. It's not like they're asking to take him out-city. It's only the...the 'Vi-park." Her voice trembles slightly, then firms.

"Well," Philip sounds grim. "We can try it this once. Make sure your communicator is fully charged in case we need to call the cops."

"Oh, darling, I'm *sure* we won't need to call the cops!" Susannah sounds genuine, making me want to hug her again. "Anyway, you'd better get Harry to Mass or you'll be late. I'll be ready to go when you get back. Harry said we need to bring our own mugs and folding chairs if we have any. That's what hunters do when they socialize."

I struggle to appreciate Mass quite as much as usual, though I try. Saint Des got me a lunch invitation, after all! But it feels a million years long. Afterward, I just have time to tell Darryl where I'm off to. Susannah phoned Ms. Williamson to change the standard lunch invitation to a dinner one, but she didn't give details about why.

Darryl grins, looking unsurprised. "Have fun."

"I wish you could come."

"Well, no-can-do." With a forced smile, she hurries away toward the bus stop to the zoo. I should've kept that stupid comment to myself. Of course she'd like to come too.

It's hard to feel down, though, as we turn into the 'Vi-park in the little Jefford city-car that feels even smaller than usual as it passes through a gateway designed for huge Habitat Vehicles. I lean forward, peering through the unobstructed windshield. At the far end of the park is a little shelter, where four HabVis are parked, two on each side.

"There, that's Technicolor, West's 'Vi. We're probably using the shelter." Good, it's a scorching hot day. "Just drive on down there and park beside the..." For a moment I grope for identifying features, realizing the four vehicles probably look near-identical to city-eyes. "...beside that right-hand 'Vi. That's Technicolor."

"How many people will there be?" asks Susannah nervously.

"Depends. I'm guessing the other 'Vis are Harmans, Trudi's folks, unless someone else turned up who got invited. The Harmans are a real large, influential clan. They run eight HabVis, I think West said once, and they've got three Elders among their older folk."

A couple of HabVis are parked at the other end of the asphalt, presumably not taking part. Guys who don't get on with the Harmans, maybe—or city-borns. Sometimes city-borns aren't invited to hunter-born stuff—and sometimes they don't want to go even when they are, to hear Josh tell it.

The group gathered around the mouth of the shelter tends heavily to dark, dark skin, so I'm guessing I'm right about Trudi's clan being well-represented. I spot Ed's pale skin and Thiago's warm brown as we pull to a halt, and I jump out quickly to cries of, "Hey, cub, long time no see!"

Ed gives me a big hug and Thiago a quick one, then they smile and shake hands with Susannah and Philip. Hand-shaking is a very city-thing, so they're clearly trying hard to make them feel welcome. West and Trudi come over and soon they're introducing everyone else. I can't keep track of everyone. All three *are* Harman 'Vis, with at least one Harman on board each—one an Elder—along with two Harman boys my age, a slightly older, unrelated boy who's apprenticed, and at least two unrelated grown-up assistants. A normal sort of mix, from what I've picked up from Josh and Technicolor over the previous year.

Susannah and Philip look quietly overwhelmed, but Trudi is quick to get them drinks and settle them where they don't have to try to talk to everyone at once. She and Elder Harman and another senior Harman keep them company while West hurries to check on the grill, from which tasty, meaty smells are wafting. Triceratops steaks and burgers, from the mouth-watering aroma.

"Harry, wanna join us?" One of the three boys waves a catapult at me.

Susannah and Philip tense in alarm, but when every other adult in sight looks on with complete unconcern, they relax a little and don't say anything. Out-city, boys my age—not *kids*, in hunter-speak, but *cubs*, old enough to hunt—would be hitting targets with rifles, not catapults—but the city-authorities would have a fit if we started shooting cans in the 'Vi-park.

"Sure." I used to mess around with a catapult when I was little. Can I still hit my mark? It looks like a standard design, a forked branch with some old innertube. Hopefully I won't disgrace myself.

We use a handy post as a target and I don't finish last—okay, I finish third—but I'm satisfied with that as West calls that the food's done.

I catch up with Technicolor about their new camp while we eat, though I try to include Susannah and Philip in the conversation too.

"It sure is good to have a family home," West remarks, as Thiago and Ed nod agreement.

"But, uh," Philip looks doubtfully from West to Thiago to Ed. "I'm guessing you three aren't...actually related?"

They laugh. "Not blood-related," says West. "Just

like-family family."

Susannah and Philip smile politely, clearly still a little confused.

"See, we own that nice HabVi on the end together." West points toward Technicolor, taking pity on their confusion. "So that makes us co-owners. Now, co-owning can just be business and it's fairly straightforward to sell your share if you wanna. Your co-owners have to agree to the buyer, but if it ain't working out between you all, they probably will. But if you co-own long enough and get along, 'specially if you're full-time 'Vi-dwellers, you'll probably end up considering yourself *like-family*."

"Is that, um, an official thing?" asks Philip.

I manage not to roll my eyes at his city obsession with officialness, though I'm listening with interest myself. Our time with Josh has made it clear there's a complicated interplay in hunter-life between business and 'Vi and camp and clan and family that I'm not even close to understanding yet.

West looks vaguely confused. "Well, if you buy a camp together, I guess it's a firmer thing. And you'd better only do *that* if you're *like-family*, 'cause it's all so much more complicated if it don't work out. If you own the controlling share in a *camp*, you can't even sell it without not only your co-owners, but everyone with camp rights, getting a vote on the new camp boss.

Whole lotta trouble."

"Camp rights?" says Susannah.

"A right to set up a permanent home in a camp, mebbe with a family, too. My dad has camp rights in another camp; him and my mom could've lived there until they died, except they've moved to our camp now so they're not exercising them anymore. It's a benefit usually earned or negotiated by long-term assistants, but sometimes given. Harry and Darryl are *like-family* with a guy who's *like-family* with us, real close. We'd give him camp rights in an instant, if he asked for them."

"So, is Harry, uh, *like-family* to you three?" asks Susannah, frowning as she tries to work it all out.

"Distantly, sure, through our…mutual family member. And Technicolor are *like-family* to the Harman clan now, 'cause I married Trudi, and that cub there that's apprenticed is a distant cousin of some Harman or other, and the two assistants here have Harman camp rights, and Harry seems to like you guys okay so I guess you're at least slightly *like-family* to him now—so I guess everyone here today is family to some degree."

Susannah and Philip eye the group of hunters, smiling nervously in response to this unexpected idea. But Susannah's cheeks go pink, and I'm not sure she minds.

I can't help eyeing everyone. I think of West and the

others as Josh's friends—his almost-uncles—not ours. But are they ours, now, too, because Josh is our family? I kinda thought looking out for me and Darryl a little might be making them feel better about the fact that they can't go near Josh, but maybe it's more than that. Hunters are very loyal to anyone within their circle, I do know that.

Talk turns to hunting tales, but everyone keeps them tame, thank God, and Susannah and Philip never look more than mildly alarmed—though even that makes people grin. Good-naturedly. Hopefully Philip's feeling real silly about his cop remark. What was he expecting? Bare knuckle brawling? More likely in a city-bar than a hunter gathering, what with Saint Des's views on fighting.

"Can they see inside Technicolor?" I ask, once we've polished off big bowls of ice cream.

"They sure can," says West. "Got something to show you, actually, Harry."

"Have you? Is it alive?" I glance at Ed.

"It were the last time I saw it," Ed replies.

"It'd better be," says Thiago, with his usual lack of optimism, "after all the time you've spent training it this last month."

There's another HabVi in the 'Vi-park, I've realized by now, swaddled in tarps and parked right in the furthermost corner. I stare at it again as we move toward Technicolor. The silhouette is eerily familiar.

West ducks his head to speak softly to me. "Yeah, that's the Wilson 'Vi. The city-folk parked it there and put big clamps on the wheels, the way they do when a sole owner is in prison. Don't worry, we drained down the water and oil, disconnected the battery and wrapped it up well. It'll be right as rain for Josh when he gets out."

I shiver slightly and hurry on to Technicolor. Suddenly I'm glad Darryl isn't here. It's horrible to see our happy home all desolate and abandoned like that. But at least West and the others have been taking care of it for Josh.

Susannah's wearing a loose summer skirt, but with Philip steadying her she manages to use the footholds and climb up into the high vehicle.

"This is the living area," I say. "But I'd better let Technicolor give the tour or they'll probably throw me out!"

West, Thiago, and Ed oblige, though it's a less detailed tour than Ed gave me the first time I entered the vehicle. Guess they can tell a lot of it would be lost on their audience. Susannah and Philip seem to find it interesting, anyway, peering around in wide-eyed curiosity.

I can't help glancing at the occupied critter cage a few times. What's in there that needs so much training?

Ed's usually got something small and furry around, although he's also a competent 'saur tamer, though not as good as Josh. But no one's as good as Josh. The Raptor Whisperer, a lot of hunters call him.

"So, that's our 'Vi," concludes West. "Until recently, I would've said *our happy home*, but now we've set up our own camp, it'll gradually become a mere work vehicle full of memories. Anyway"—West hits the button to close the side door—"We've got a real nice critter to show you. *Mus ficedulusaur*." He gives me a tiny wink as Ed goes to open the cage.

A *what?* But it seems best to go along with it. Since when do hunters use an animal's Latin name?

Oh. That's why. Ed turns around holding a rodento'saur in his arms. He sets it down on the folding table, allowing me to see it better. It's a healthy young male, a trace of nestling down still visible under its sleek grey-black juvenile plumage. He cocks his head to look at us all, seeming unalarmed. Rodento'saurs are about the same height as a piranha'saur, about twelve inches, but have stockier bodies—less neck and tail— with much stronger jaws, and they're feathered as adults. Neither species sport the massive killing claws of the raptor family, giving them a less intimidating appearance.

"He's a gorgeous, er..." I trail off.

"*Mus ficedulusaur*," supplies Ed, straight-faced,

avoiding the name well-known to put off city-folk.

"Oh yeah. Can I handle him?"

"Sure can. He's tamed, trained, and house-broken. Ready to go to a nice city-home."

That's what Thiago meant about the training time. I had piranha'saurs when I was a kid, which are super popular but real one-person pets. Rodento'saurs, Josh taught us, make far better pets once they're tamed because they'll be nice to everyone in the family, not just the one who feeds them. But shy rodos are slower to tame and their stronger bite means pet shops can't just sell them untamed and leave it to their new owners, the way they often do with piranha'saurs. They're more expensive to prepare for the market, basically—and their name is a problem—so despite their advantages they're not common.

I can't help glancing from West to Ed, wondering. Could this critter be meant for...for *me*? It's exactly the right pet to share a house with Susannah and Philip. It won't bite them, and like most critters that naturally spend a lot of time down tunnels, it will even use a litterbox. And sleep the day away while I'm at school.

"Hello, boy..." I hold out my hand for the *Mus-* whatever to sniff.

"Oh, Harry, careful, is it safe?" Susannah blurts.

"If Ed says it's tame, it's tame," I say confidently, as Ed slips some treats into my other hand.

The rodento'saur cocks its head, staring expectantly at me with bright beady eyes. "What's he called?"

"Perky," say Ed.

I laugh. "Perfect. Hi, Perky. I know what you want..." I hold out a treat on my hand and Perky takes it as politely as Susannah could wish, no wild grabbing. "Good boy."

I stroke his chest, letting him sniff me some more before moving on to his back. "Can I pick you up, little fella? Good boy, there we go."

Perky balances himself against my chest with a wing-arm and looks around alertly, clearly unconcerned. "See, he's very tame," I tell Susannah, taking a few steps to her. "You can stroke him if you like."

"It's got very sharp-looking teeth. What does it eat?"

"This and that. It's an omnivore." Quite a meat-heavy omnivore, but definitely an omnivore, I'm not lying.

Cautiously, Susannah strokes Perky on his back, almost on his tail, well away from his toothy end. "He's nice and soft."

"Yeah, can you feel the fluff underneath?" I tell her. "That's the last of his nestling down. And the sleek feathers on top are his juvenile plumage. Next spring he'll grow adult plumage instead, fancier than this since he's male, though not fancy like some species have."

Susannah strokes Perky some more, freezing when he ducks his head to sniff her hand, then relaxing and getting more bold when he just cocks his head at her and does nothing else.

"You're a nice boy," she murmurs, stroking his neck. "It's as good as being at the zoo, Philip!"

When Philip cautiously reaches out to feel the soft feathers as well, West winks at me again, making hope explode in my chest. Perky *is* for me, isn't he? Please let him be for me... Please let Susannah and Philip say yes!

"Wanna see something cool?" says West, once Susannah and Philip have had a few minutes to bond with Perky—I hope!

"What?" I ask.

Thiago's just produced a light from a cupboard and plugged it in over the table. It produces a strange purple light. "What's that?"

"UV," Thiago says. "Let's take a look at Perky, shall we? Lights, Ed?"

When I carry Perky over and set him down under the purple light, Ed switches off the main interior lights.

"Wow!" I exclaim.

Philip and Susannah gasp.

"That ain't nothing," says Ed. "Wait until he's into his adult plumage."

Perky's drab black-grey coat has been transformed

into a gorgeous purple with shimmering highlights. "That *is* cool. I think—" I break off. *I think Josh mentioned something about UV,* I was going to say, but I know I can't mention Josh. Don't want to get Technicolor in trouble.

"A lot of 'saurs—and birds, too—look real fancy under UV," says Thiago. "They can see that kinda light, you know. So, some of the male feathered 'saurs you think don't have display plumage—think again. Oftentimes humans just can't see it."

"I always think anyone who owns one of these should have a UV bulb in a lamp in their living room," he adds. "Then whenever their pet runs under it, they—and their visitors—get to enjoy...*this.*" He gestures to where Perky still shimmers under the light, cocking his head at us as though wondering what all the fuss is about.

I could clap my hands together with glee. Susannah and Philip sure do like their smart city decor. Surely the thought of a living decoration this rare and fine will be attractive to them?

After giving us a few more minutes to admire Perky's hidden beauty, Ed switches the lights back on. "Elder Harman said something about marshmallows," he remarks. "I reckon we should get back out there before they're all gone."

"You big kid," says Thiago.

"We both know you'll eat more than me," says Ed, unruffled. "Dunno how you stay so skinny."

I glance at West, my heart in my mouth, but his eyelid simply shivers in another, tiny wink. *Patience.* Right. We need Susannah and Ed to be as familiar and comfortable with Perky as they possibly can be before we ask them.

"Can Perky come out with us?"

"Sure." Ed places a harness and leash he's just taken from a cupboard onto the table. "He's all leash-trained; just buckle him in."

Perky submits to the harness without any protest. Ed sure has done a good job with him. He hasn't done a single thing to put Susannah or Philip off, yet.

But will it be enough?

DARRYL

Even the zoo doesn't lift my spirits quite as much as normal, as I picture Harry at the 'Vi-park, having a great time with Technicolor. I definitely don't begrudge him—I'd just so love to be there too. But I can't go anywhere near hunters or country-folk. Not without 'good cause.'

I sigh and try to put it from my mind again as I watch the velociraptors. The chicks are young juveniles, now, roaming everywhere, getting into everything, insatiably curious. The chill zoo-raptor parents have practically given up keeping more than a cursory eye on them. No predators. Why worry?

They've got a well-set-up habitat. A pool and stream. A salt and mineral lick. Fresh tree branches strewn around for chewing and scratching and nibbling at. Heat lamps are visible in the nursery caves, though they're not on in this warm summer weather. Feeding time, soon.

My heart still feels heavy, though. Thoughts of The Plan—the now unlikely-to-succeed Plan—creep back into my head yet again. Trying to shake them away, I start on a Chaplet of Saint Desmond as the raptors idle around below.

By the time I've finished, they're looking less idle, heads up, watching the gates where the prey may emerge. The ObsoDeck has filled up with eager visitors, waiting to see the mice meet their fate. On weekdays, the velociraptors get a small pig or a small pygmy goat once a day, but on the weekend it's very small prey, several times each day, to reduce the crush on the ObsoDeck at feeding times. Mice for the velociraptors, rats for the Dakotas, and rabbits for the Utahraptors.

Squeak. A gate slides up and about ten—huh, *rats,* today—spill into the paddock. The rats scatter—so do the velociraptors. Hisses and squeals from both predators and prey as they try to escape or scuffle over a meal.

One of the juveniles—the one the public named Super Soaker for some incomprehensible reason but which I just call Super—has grabbed a particularly large rat, killing it with a quick bite. Tossing it up into the air, he begins to swallow it, throat working hard. "That's too big for you, silly," I mutter. "Didn't your mother teach you to chew your food?"

Although swallowing whole is their preferred way of ingesting smaller pray, raptors can't unhinge their jaws like snakes, nor do their gullets stretch the same way, so there's a definite limit to what they can cope with.

"Come on, Super, spit it out and eat it properly," I murmur, as the silly beast continues to gulp greedily, trying to get it down. Probably afraid a sibling will steal it if he tries to eat it the slow way, not that he'll be *hungry*-hungry. Zoo-raptor, after all.

Most of the rats have been caught now. The adults are already flopping down again in a lazy heap and beginning mutual preening to remove blood smell. Even life in the zoo can't eradicate that deep-seated instinct.

The juveniles bounce around, still over-excited. Except...*outage*, Super hasn't spat that rat back out. He's *trying*, whipping his head from side to side as his chest and throat heave violently, but he can't get rid of it.

"Ugh, you silly beast!" I watch, worried.

He's got his head on the ground, now, trying to catch at the rat's tail with his wing-claws, to pull it out, but he can't get a grip on the thin, slippery thing.

I don't wait any longer. Better a red face for raising a false alarm... "Hey!" I yell, trying to make myself heard over the noise of the oblivious crowd. "Hey, paddock attendant, we need a keeper! We need a keeper *now!*"

He's not listening. Maybe can't even *hear* me.

The juvenile staggers, head hanging. His struggles are getting weaker. He's suffocating, right enough.

"Somebody get a keeper!" I yell. Can I push my way to the attendant; get him to use his walkie-talkie?

Super collapses on the ground, claws scrabbling feebly in the dirt. *Outage! No time!*

I vault over the fence, onto the overhang, and jump down into the paddock.

Guess I'll have to deal with it myself!

HARRY

"That's a real nice rodo," says Elder Harman's grandson, so admiringly that I wonder if he's been coached in advance by Technicolor. "Chill temperament."

"Sure is," I agree, watching Perky scampering back

up to me on his leash, hoping for a treat.

"Yeah," agrees Ed, nodding. "That little fella is gonna make some boy or girl very happy indeed. And the adults, too. A real nice, well-trained *Mus ficedulusaur* is a wonderful addition to a family."

West nods too. "Best family pet, I'd say."

I pat my lap, rewarding Perky with a treat when he leaps straight up. "There you go."

Uh-oh, that latest listing of the virtues of *Mus ficedulusaur* has brought a wary look to Susannah's eye. Has she figured out where this is all headed?

Thankfully, she keeps quiet, even letting him sit on her lap for a while as one of the Harmans gets out some drums and we sing for a while, popular songs and hunter ballads and some hymns too.

Susannah and Philip don't seem in a hurry to leave, so they must be enjoying themselves well enough. The longer they spend chilling with Perky, the better. I keep encouraging him to interact with them as subtly as I can. Oh, I really want to keep him! Having Dad and the farm and Josh and, even to some extent, Darryl snatched away has left a horrible void inside for months and Perky's jumped right into it. He can't possibly fill it, but he makes it a little warmer and less empty. Eventually, West's gonna offer him to me, I know he is.

But I don't know what they're gonna say!

DARRYL

I dash over to where Super lies limp on the ground, quickly straddling him and pressing my knees to his sides to control both his legs and wing arms, both of which have claws I don't wish to tangle with. Grabbing the back of his head with one hand and holding on as firmly as I can, both for my own safety and to have something to pull against, I grip the rat's tail and try to draw it out. Yep, it's wedged in there, alright.

The tail slides through my fingers, so I wrap it around two of them several times and try again. Good, that's giving me more grip. Is it moving? Maybe. I increase the pressure, trying to keep a steady pull to reduce the chances of damaging Super's gullet.

Is it...is it...yes, it's coming. Carefully, I draw the rat all the way out and hurl it to the far end of the pen, hoping to draw the pack away. Super gives a massive gasp and begins to pant violently, his eyes dazed.

A menacing hiss from far too close...slowly, avoiding sudden movements, I look up.

So much for the rat.

The matriarch stands feet away, head lowered, yellow ruff flaring, tail whipping high behind her. All signs of aggression. Uh-oh, Super's one of her chicks, isn't he?

Behind her, her silky-feathered mate stares at me in a puzzled manner, as though wondering what I'm doing in the paddock but giving me the benefit of the doubt as far as the gasping chick is concerned. Was he hand-reared or something? No, the info board said he was wild-caught.

I push the question away. I've got bigger things to worry about.

Slowly, carefully, I ease myself off Super, getting as far back as I can before releasing his head. But I needn't have worried about *him*; he just sits there, far too weak and shocked after his near-miss to be interested in me.

The matriarch—Banana, she's called—is another matter. Fortunately, as I keep backing slowly toward the paddock wall, she pauses to check on Super. From her level of anxiety, maybe she realized he was in trouble before I managed to get to him. I kinda hope so. Silky comes forward to inspect the chick too, and Banana takes a few steps toward me. Uh-oh.

I risk a few quick glances around the paddock, checking on the other raptors. Most of them are scuffling over the last shreds of the rat I threw, but a few are staring and moving my way. Quickly, I unbutton the blouse I threw over my t-shirt for sun protection and hold it wide open, making myself look larger.

"Now, I was only helping him, Banana," I say in a loud, confident voice. "So don't you get silly with me. Not when I'm so much bigger than you. See how huge I am?" I do my best to loom, both physically and psychologically.

She stands, head to one side, staring up at me. Not attacking. She looks back at where Silky still nuzzles a whimpering Super, then at me.

Is it possible she understands that I helped him?

Or does she assume I'm the reason he's in that state?

I keep inching carefully backwards, getting closer and closer to the nearest gate. I don't even need to glance up at that overhang. If it will keep a velociraptor down here, it will stop me. Banana follows, head up — rather than down in a hunting posture — eyes fixed to me.

"Yes, that's right, I helped him, so you play nice," I keep repeating, very firmly indeed.

That stick there would make a good weapon — so I push it along behind me to keep it within reach.

The rest of the pack bound toward us, eyes fixed to me, but I don't dare back up any faster. Even if she does realize that I helped her chick, she may not remember it for long, and the slightest hint of prey behavior from me could snap whatever understanding we may — or may not — have going on. She's the matriarch — if she goes for me, they all will.

The other raptors form a semi-circle around me, heads low, tails whisking with excitement at the novelty of my presence, staring curiously—and warily. I'm a lot bigger than they are and I'm something that—while familiar—doesn't usually come close to them. I go up on tip-toe to look even larger still, keeping my blouse high and wide, rumbling loudly—my best impression of an irritable allosaur—though not loudly or aggressively enough to provoke a preemptive attack. If they come for me, I need to let go my blouse and cover my neck and stomach *at once*, while grabbing the stick—but unless they do, it's better to look bigger and concentrate on warning them off.

The other raptors keep glancing at their matriarch but, thankfully, Banana still doesn't attack. She *must* know I was helping the chick. Silky, her mate, actually chirps hopefully at me, as though wondering if I have treats.

I step back a few more paces—and feel the gate behind me.

"Could someone let me out?" I say in the same loud, firm voice I've been using.

It's already squeaking up. I step back through it...*squeak*. Down it goes.

"Well, I sure am glad to be out of there," I tell the guy standing by the controls. "Even a slight risk of becoming a chew-toy for that bunch isn't fun."

It's the middle-aged keeper I met before. Ned, was it? He's staring down at me, his pale skin even paler than before.

"What were you thinking, going into that pen?"

"Your chick—well, juvenile—was choking to death, didn't you see?"

"I arrived in time to see you doing something to one of them with remarkable competence, couldn't see what."

"Extracting the meal he'd about finished choking to death on, was what. Why are you feeding the velociraptors *rats* when their chicks are still this small?"

"Rats?" A look of fury crosses his face and he mutters, "I'll give him *rats*. That is *it!*" but his eyes move straight back to me. "You're *absolutely sure* you're okay?"

"Fine. They didn't get anywhere near me."

"Heck, I haven't had a fright like that since our raptor consultant jumped into a pen with an allo to save a little girl the other year. Ten minutes that took ten years off my life, I tell you!"

Sounds like something Josh would do, that does!

"You shouldn't have gone in, choking chick or no chick," he adds. "You could've been badly hurt."

"Well, they were only velociraptors. You can bet if they were Dakota or Utah—or an allo, God forbid!— you'd have one less chick right now."

"*Only velociraptors?*" He shakes his head. "Well, you knew how to handle them, I give you that. You extracted yourself, textbook perfect."

I shrug. "I was trained by an expert."

Ned sighs. "That raptor expert we use has gotten himself chucked in prison for a stretch, can you believe? Nicest guy imaginable, some minor trouble over a girl; I trust they'll let him out soon."

I try not to let my eyes widen. It *was* Josh! Heck, that's a tale he's never told. An *allo*?

He stares thoughtfully at me. "You didn't pick up the stick."

I can't help laughing. "Of course I didn't pick up the stick. With me being so much larger and so unfamiliar, and the gate so close, the odds were very high I could control the situation long enough to extract myself—but the instant I crouched for that stick they'd have been on me, like as not, and it would've turned into a fight. As long as the matriarch held off, the stick was just a dangerous distraction."

He nods. "True, every word, but I don't know many people who could have resisted grabbing it. *Odds*, huh? Are you a hunter, did you say?"

"Farmer-born, hunter-trained."

"Well, I'd say an internship is yours if you want it, after what I've just seen. No need to go through the application process."

I stare at him as my brain catches up with what he's just said, then my heart wrings itself out with longing.

It's looking increasingly likely I'll have to spend the next three years in-city no matter what, and I could spend them working *here*? But no. Sure, the internship is one of the most 'desirable' career jobs imaginable. But it's also three years long and at no point during that time will I be able to afford to keep Harry. And once Harry's eighteen, we'll be going to the farm. If I take it, I not only give up all hope of getting custody, but I deprive some city-kid who really wants a zoo career of their one chance.

I shake my head heavily. "Sorry. I just can't afford to keep my kid brother on an internship. I have to say no."

"Oh, yeah, you mentioned a brother." He eyes me some more. "Who trained you?"

I moisten my lips nervously. "Uh...Joshua Wilson."

His eyes widen, then he grins. "You're the girl." It isn't a question.

I shrug. "It wasn't like that, but yeah, I'm afraid it is kinda my fault your raptor consultant is locked up."

"Okay, if *he* trained you, now I've *got* to have you on my staff." A sudden look of glee enters his eyes. "Well, now, I'd say junior sub-keepers at zoos get paid enough to keep a kid brother, if neither of them have expensive tastes. And it happens there's a lazy sloth who I've told three separate times not to feed rats to the velociraptors just yet who's clearing his locker this afternoon. You can have his job. Only seems fair."

I stare at him, my heart in my mouth. "Are you teasing me, sir? Please don't tease me, you have *no idea* what that job would mean—"

"I'm not teasing, girl. I'm not that cruel. Do you want it?"

I hesitate as another thought crosses my mind. "Is there a...a contract period?"

"Three months probation, then after that just a normal one month's notice. It's not hard to replace zoo staff, trust me."

Relief floods me. I can work at the zoo until I get custody—and you bet I'll get custody, they'd never *dream* I'd give up a *zoo job* to go out-city—and then we can go home! "Then yes! And thank you!"

He eyes me. "Might not have you for all that long, huh? Well, I'm smart enough to take what I can get while I can get it. Can you start tomorrow?"

I nod, then frown. "Oh, I'm not eighteen for another week."

He waves that away. "Come along to the carni'saur handling complex at ten. We'll have finished morning chores by then, so I can get you inducted. I'm Ned Greyson, head raptor keeper, by the way."

"Darryl Franklyn."

"Very pleased to have you. Now, are you—"

"I really am fine."

"Ah, yes." With a wry smile, he gestures for me to precede him into the passageway just as a bunch of other keepers come panting—belatedly—around the corner, clutching rifles. "*Only* velociraptors. I forgot."

HARRY

By the time we've finished the singing and cooked some more marshmallows and the older hunters have told more—unusually tame—tales, Perky has curled up in my lap and fallen asleep—to my delight. It would hardly be surprising if he preferred Ed's company. But Ed's been staying clear, and I've been careful to give Perky plenty of treats and attention.

"Well..." Philip is checking the time. My gut clenches up. The moment I've been dreading and waiting for has come! "We'd probably better get going. My, yes, it's almost five."

"Thank you for a lovely lunch," Susannah says. "It's been such a nice afternoon."

"Good to have you," says West.

"And great to see Harry," says Ed.

"He's a good cub," says Thiago, making me smile, since Thiago isn't usually very free with his praise.

"Oh, uh"—West pauses them as they begin to rise—"What would you say to Harry keeping Perky? They seem to have taken to each other real well."

Philip's jaw drops open—Susannah barely blinks. "I expect that would be okay." She glances at Philip. "Don't you think, Philip?"

"Uh..." He directs a pleading look at her—she just stares back. "Oh, sure. Fine. It *is* litterbox trained, right? That is what you said?"

"Oh course." Ed nods.

"Harry, you will need to deal with all that," says Philip, eyeing me firmly. "Your pet; your responsibility."

I'm not sure whether to laugh or scowl, since I've been trying to persuade them to give me *responsibility* for months. I manage to simply nod. "Of course."

And then—unbelievably, after months of everything going wrong—I'm getting into the car with my wonderful new pet. I can't wait to show him to Darryl tonight.

Susannah and Philip murmur polite hints about how we must do this again sometime and the hunters agree, far more directly. I think Susannah and Philip mean it, *yes, yes, yes!*

Philip slams his car door at last as everyone else returns to the shelter with final waves over their shoulders. "So this, uh, *mus f...*" Philip trails off, tripping over his tongue.

"It's a *rodento'saur*, dear," says Susannah, making him do a double-take into the back seat.

"Most people just call them rodos," I say quickly.

Fortunately he just sighs, shakes his head, muttering something about sly hunters, and puts the car in drive. *Yes!* Perky is mine.

"It sounded to me," he says, as we pull away, "as though the, er, *rodo* was worth quite a lot. You've got good friends, Harry. Or, er, distant *like-family*, is it?"

"Yeah, I do." Not hard to sound grateful. Knowing all those hunters consider me *like-family*, even distantly, makes me feel much less alone, too.

Perky curls up in my lap again and goes back to sleep. Rodos are only primarily nocturnal, they're quite capable of being awake part of the day, but he's clearly tired after all the stimulation. I stroke him as we drive along, happiness swelling me up like an over-filled balloon. Even with the now-so-unlikely best-case scenario, I'll still be in-city for several more months.

But at least I have a little friend of my very own—and a lot more family than I knew anything about. And foster-parents who'll let me keep the one—and see the other.

DARRYL

I'm crawling through deep snow on all fours. How did I end up outside the 'Vi? In this? Icy flakes lash my face like a whip. Every time I drag one chilling limb free, another sinks even further. The slope's getting steeper. I'm beginning to slide back down it, and the snow's sucking me down like quicksand, deeper and deeper...

"Darryl, here!"

Josh leans from clear, solid rock, reaching out. I catch hold of his hand and he heaves, dragging me free. I stand beside him, shaking.

"Thanks!"

"It was only an allo."

"What?" But Josh is gone. "Josh? Josh?"

I start running, panicking, floundering through the snow, searching for him. Where is he? Did something snatch him? He was just there beside me—wasn't he?

"Josh!" No answer. Blind panic fills me... "JOSH!"

I'm running over grassland now, pasture that looks much like the area I grew up in, the area around our farm... What happened to the snow?

"Darryl?" The voice comes faintly.

"Josh?" I run toward the voice, and suddenly I'm inside a dark cave, stumbling over rough stony ground. "Josh?"

"Darryl?" It's not Josh's voice. It's...

"Dad?" I dash forward, only to jerk to a halt, teetering on the edge of a deep pit. "Dad?"

I drop to hands and knees, staring down. Despite the darkness, I can see Dad quite clearly, crouched at the bottom.

"Darryl, help me!"

"Wait, Dad, I'll...I'll lower a rope."

The only thing to fasten the rope to is a metal ring. I put the rope through it and drop both ends down. "Hold both strands tightly," I call to him. "It's not tied on."

Shouldn't I tie it? But it doesn't seem a good idea.

Dad grabs the rope, just one strand, and starts pulling it.

"No, Dad, you need to hold both—"

He ignores me, pulling steadily until the end of the rope whisks through the ring and drops into the pit, just ahead of my grab. "Dad, no! How are you going to get it back up here now?"

He crouches again. "Darryl, help me!"

"I'm trying, Dad! Why did you pull the rope down?"

"You've got to help me!"

"I will, but I need another rope. And...and I need to find Josh." Yes, I was looking for Josh, wasn't I? Dad's safe in the pit for now. Maybe I should look for Josh some more...

"Darryl, help me..."

Hands thrust between my shoulder blades, hard, and I topple over the edge, a whiff of familiar perfume in my nostrils.

Falling—

I jerk awake, gasping. Sitting up in the bunk I'll be leaving in just a few more days, I shudder. It was such a nice day yesterday, what with getting that perfect job and Harry being given that lovely little fella, Perky— that was real nice of Technicolor. Shame to follow it up with such a horrible dream. Sweat soaks my pajamas.

Still, it was just a nightmare, right? From all the excitement, maybe. In fact, it was real nice to see Josh—until he disappeared. I still don't have a photo of him.

I lie back down, staring up at the ceiling. I haven't thought about Dad so much, recently. Mostly just in the evening, when I often look through my photo album before bed. Honestly? I think about Josh way more. Heck, I miss him. And I worry about Harry, a lot.

Dad is dead. We had the Mass, finally. The police aren't pursuing the case. Dad's dead, and I thought I'd come to terms with the fact we'd never be burying him. So why am I dreaming about him?

Am I belatedly feeling guilty because we've stopped looking for him? But there's nothing wrong with stopping looking for a dead man, right?

A cold draft touches my sweaty skin and with it comes a little voice in my head, asking a question I've not asked myself for months.

What if Dad isn't *dead?*

Yet.

+

Missing Josh too?
Read unSPARKed 9:
A Different Kind of Freedom

DID YOU MISS ANY BOOKS?
PICK THEM UP TODAY!

DON'T FORGET THE PREQUELS!

DO CARPENTERS DREAM OF WOODEN SHEEP?

+

THE NATIVITY STORY— WITH A SCI-FI TWIST!

Razim's staying overnight to help his friend Daniel, who's sick with leukaemia, but he's forgotten his phone! Lying awake after watching Blade Runner, Razim reads the only story he can find—about Joseph and Mary—only to fall asleep and find himself in futuristic Merillia.

In Merillia, his name is Cleopas, and his big brother, Jo, is considering an arranged marriage to a girl called Miryam. Soon, events are in motion that will change their lives—and the world—forever.

For anyone who feels over-familiar with the story of St. Joseph and the Holy Family after Christmas after Christmas of nativity plays, this imaginative re-telling thoroughly blows the dust off.

This standalone story can be read on its own or in between books 1 and 2 of Corinna Turner's 'Friends in High Places' series.

"It's difficult to re-tell such an overly familiar story like Joseph's and the Nativity story, but this creative adaption gives it a fresh twist!"
CAROLYN ASTFALK, author of Rightfully Ours

Turn over for a SNEAK PEEK!

DO CARPENTERS DREAM OF WOODEN SHEEP?
Sneak Peek

"I can't believe you're going through with this." I raise my voice over the sound of a hover-bus passing too close over the top of our ancient domestic pod.

Jo carefully straightens the colorful wide sash that's been part of Merillian formal wear for centuries, even though it's falling out of use in favor of Imperial fashions, nowadays. "Why? It's traditional."

"Yeah, but you don't have to anymore. That's a freedom the Empire actually has brought."

Jo shoots me a look of amusement. "It's an arranged marriage, little bro, not a forced marriage. Big diff. And it's not like the way it used to be done. All we're doing today is getting introduced. Then we get to know each other, and only then do we decide whether we want to go ahead and get married."

"I still don't see why you don't just find a girl for yourself."

"Because the matchmaker has spent decades learning who's likely to be compatible with whom. So I might as well give this a try first, right?"

When he puts it like that, it doesn't sound so dumb, not if you're looking for marriage and no sordid messing around, which is definitely what my big brother is after. Some people use the info-xchange to find girlfriends, after all. Probably better to trust your future happiness to a person than to a machine.

"Well, I've got your back, whatever you decide."

He grins at me. "Thanks, Cleo." He fidgets with his sash again. He's more nervous than he's letting on.

"You look good," I tell him. "She'll swoon."

"Ah, very funny." But he looks fractionally more relaxed as he heads for the broken up-down conveyer. Not for the first time, as we trek downstairs, I wonder what it's like to live in a domestic pod where everything works. Jo swears that when I was very young, when Amma and Abba were both still alive and had recently moved here from Bethlasa, our pod was all in proper order, like other people's. But I don't remember. I barely even remember them. Jo's been keeping us with his woodcarving since forever.

At least now I'm old enough to have my hover-permit, I can do delivery work and make some money too. Seeing that I'm rubbish at carving. I'm good at fixing things, but you have to be careful, showing serious skills. Imperial soldiers get a bounty for every conscript they sign up, which is why they get so rough about it—but if they sign up someone skilled, they get double. They don't need carpenters—wood goods are for decoration—but engineers? I'm better off delivering stuff, even if the pay is low.

Sealing the pod behind us, we climb into the hover-van I managed to scrape together enough to buy and we're off through the streets to the matchmaker's.

"Okay," I say, parking two doors down, under a lurid flickering neon sign. "Time to meet your fate."

"Very funny," says Jo. Sweating. Well, he decided to do this.

We keep a careful lookout for swipe-thieves, regional

security forces, or imperial soldiers as we walk the short distance to the matchmaker's door. The first will beat you and take your valuables, the second will frisk you in a more official manner but make your stuff disappear just as fast, and the third might do either—or worse, conscript you on the spot.

In we go. The up-down here works, and soon we're being shown into the matchmaker's receiving room. Oh boy…the prospective bride is already here, standing between her elderly parents with her head bowed. They look old enough to drop off their perches any time, in fact. Is that why she's put herself up for an arranged marriage? If they've got nothing to leave her…well, it's hard for a woman to survive alone. Between Imperial taxes and the Regional Supreme Leader's whims and the dangerous streets… Well, that doesn't matter, if she's both nice and pretty. I guess Jo, being Jo, will only really care if she's nice. But I stare, trying to make out her face.

Jo stops and bows formally, so I do the same. Our traditions are getting forgotten fast, now we're part of the Empire, but not by Jo.

The bridal party bows as well, and finally the young woman looks up. Girl. The girl looks up. She's young, maybe sixteen, about my age, her skin smooth coffee perfection, her eyes dark and warm. And her poise…like a katachara dancer. And…and…something else about her. What is it?

Jo is staring at her as though he's been struck dumb, but the matchmaker is clearly used to this and begins some spiel of introduction that gives Jo time to pull himself together. Then I take tea with the matchmaker and the elderly parents *of the bride—Joachim and Annei—while Jo goes into the matching chamber for private refreshments with the girl herself. Miryam, her name is. Her parents are sweet and kind and doddery, and embarrassingly enthusiastic about me—even though it's Jo who's going to be marrying their daughter if it all works out—and I'm not sorry when the hour is up.*

Jo is silent as we take the up-down back to the lobby. It's up to me to keep an eye out for danger as we walk the short distance back to the hover-van. He settles into the seat silently, still staring into space.

"So?" Once my door is sealed to keep out the smog, I can't wait any longer. "What did you think of her?"

He turns his head slowly, like a man coming out of a dream, wonder in his eyes. "Did you ever…ever see anything so pure in all your life? Anyone so pure…"

Pure. Yes, that was it, the indefinable quality about Miryam. Purity. Not unlike my big brother, only—and I'd not have thought it possible—even more so. I glance at Jo's face. Oh yeah, it's a done deal, all right.

And three weeks later, Miryam and Jo become formally betrothed. Big surprise. Not.

+

I'm trying to bring a pan of seyii beans to the boil without them all leaping out of the saucepan, when Jo gets home. He seems distracted as he takes off his gatu and hangs it on the hook.

"Miryam okay?" They've been engaged for six months and he's still smitten with her—and it seems to be mutual.

"Yes," he speaks slowly.

187

"Then what's wrong? Have you finally decided to ditch the traditional one-year wait and finalize the marriage early?"

"What? No, of course not." He steps into the kitchen and makes an automatic check inside the chill-chest, though I don't think he takes in the contents. It's comfortably full, unlike its usual state when we were younger. "No, Miryam had to go visit her cousin Elizabet. I just saw her safely onto the skimmer. Zecharii will pick her up at the other end."

"How long will she be gone?"

"Several months."

"Months?" And I thought the courtship was going so well! "Did you fall out?"

"No, her cousin's having a baby. She needs Miryam's help."

"Her cousin?" My love-struck brother has filled me in on every tiny detail of the flawless Miryam and her family, and I'm pretty sure… "She's only got one cousin, right? And she's, what, sixty or something? She can't be having a baby."

"Well, she is. I think it may be some sort of miracle." Jo speaks calmly, with that quiet conviction about such things that I've always found awe-inspiring and frustrating all at once.

"You really believe that?"

"She's sixty-nine. So, yes."

I don't have an answer to that.

Get DO CARPENTERS DREAM OF WOODEN SHEEP? from your favorite retailer today!

ABOUT THE AUTHOR

Corinna Turner has been writing since she was fourteen and likes strong protagonists with plenty of integrity. Although she spends as much time as possible writing, she cannot keep up with the flow of ideas, for which she offers thanks—and occasional grumbles!—to the Holy Spirit. She is the author of over twenty-five books, including the Carnegie Medal Nominated I Am Margaret series, and her work has been translated into four languages. She was awarded the St. Katherine Drexel award in 2022.

She is a Lay Dominican with an MA in English from Oxford University and lives in the UK. She is a member of a number of organizations, including the Society of Authors, Catholic Teen Books, Catholic Reads, the Angelic Warfare Confraternity, and the Sodality of the Blessed Sacrament. She used to have a Giant African Land Snail, Peter, with a 6½" long shell, but now makes do with a cactus and a campervan.

Get in touch with Corinna...

Facebook: Corinna Turner

Twitter: @CorinnaTAuthor

Don't forget to sign up for

NEWS

&

FREE SHORT STORIES

at:

www.UnSeenBooks.com

All Free/Exclusive content subject to availability.